Sweeties

Charmz™

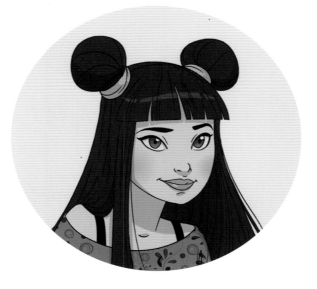

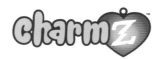

MORE GREAT GRAPHIC NOVEL SERIES FROM

charmz™

STITCHED #1 "The First Day of the Rest of Her Life"

CHLOE #1 "The New Girl"

Story by Cathy Cassidy

Written by Veronique Grisseaux

Art and colors by Anna Merle

NEW YORK

Based on the novel "The Chocolate Box Girls-Cherry Crush and Marshmallow Skye,"
by Cathy Cassidy, first published by Puffin Books (The Penguin Group, London)
The Chocolate Box Girls Cherry Crush © 2010 by Cathy Cassidy
The Chocolate Box Girls Marshmallow Skye © 2011 by Cathy Cassidy
Comics originally published in French as *Les filles au chocolat* volume 1
"Cœur cerise" © Jungle! 2014 and *Les filles au chocolat* volume 2 *"Cœur guimauve"*
© Jungle! 2015 Jungle!, Miss Jungle! and the Jungle! logo are ® 2016 Steinkis Groupe
www.editions-jungle.com

SWEETIES #1
"Cherry/Skye"

Original story: CATHY CASSIDY
Comics adaptation: VERONIQUE GRISSEAUX
Cover artwork: ANNA MERLI & RAYMOND SÉBASTIEN
Interior comics art: ANNA MERLI & CLAUDIA and MARCO
FORCELLONI, YELLOW WHALE CREATIVE STUDIOS
JOE JOHNSON — Translation
SASHA KIMIATEK — Production Coordinator
JEFF WHITMAN — Assistant Managing Editor
MARIAH McCOURT — Editor
JIM SALICRUP
Editor-in-Chief

Charmz is an imprint of Papercutz.

HC ISBN: 978-1-62991-773-3
PB ISBN: 978-1-62991-764-1

Printed in China
May 2017

Charmz books may be purchased for business or promotional use.
For information on bulk purchases please contact Macmillan
Corporate and Premium Sales Department at
(800) 221-7945 x5442

Distributed by Macmillan
First Charmz Printing

GLASGOW, SCOTLAND. CLYDE ACADEMY.

CAN'T LIE.

THERE ARE SOME THINGS I'LL MISS ABOUT CLYDE ACADEMY.

LIKE THIS *DELIGHTFUL* LUNCH FOOD.

OR STARING AT THE BACK OF RYAN CLEGG'S... NECK.

THERE ARE ALSO THINGS I WILL *NOT* MISS:

LIKE MATH TESTS AND--

KIRSTY McRAE!

SHE AND HER FRIENDS DRIVE ME CRAZY!

EXCUSE ME, CHERRY COSTELLO!

WE NEED SOME MORE ROOM.

WAP

HEY, GIRLS!

DID YOU KNOW, CHERRY'S MUM THOUGHT SHE WAS SUCH A *LOSER* THAT SHE DITCHED HER AND RAN OFF TO LIVE ON THE OTHER SIDE OF THE WORLD?

YOU DON'T KNOW ANYTHING ABOUT MY MUM!

5

OH, YES, I DO, CHERRY.

IN ELEMENTARY SCHOOL, YOU TOLD ME SHE WAS A MOVIE STAR, AND IN FIFTH GRADE, SHE WAS A FASHION DESIGNER.

YOU ARE SUCH A LIAR!

ARE YOU ADOPTED?

BECAUSE YOU DON'T LOOK ANYTHING LIKE YOUR DAD! YOU LOOK--I DUNNO, CHINESE, OR JAPANESE, OR SOMETHING.

I'M SCOTTISH! JUST LIKE DAD!

I DON'T THINK--

--HE'S YOUR DAD AT ALL!

LIKE I SAID...

I WILL NOT MISS KIRSTY McRAE.

YOU MADE UP STORIES, CHERRY, TO MAKE YOURSELF SEEM INTERESTING.

ONLY, YOU'RE NOT INTERESTING, NOT ONE BIT. AND NEITHER IS YOUR MUM.

CLAP

CLAP

CLAP

CLAP CLAP

OH. MY. GOD.

6

--POOR KIRSTY IS IN THE NURSE'S OFFICE, GETTING FIRST AID. YOU'RE LUCKY SHE DOESN'T HAVE BURNS!

MRS. JARDINE DIRECTOR

BUT-- MRS. JARDINE-- KIRSTY--

CHERRY COSTELLO, YOUR BEHAVIOR IS UNACCEPTABLE!

WHAT HAS KIRSTY McRAE EVER DONE TO YOU?

MRS. JARDINE DIRECTOR

WELL, LAST WEEK SHE FLUSHED MY GYM SOCKS DOWN THE LOO.

BUT IF I TELL MRS. JARDINE THAT, SHE WON'T BELIEVE ME.

SHE...

SHE CALLED ME A LIAR!

LIAR? WELL, THAT'S A VERY HARSH WORD. BUT YOU DO HAVE A TENDENCY TO EMBROIDER THE TRUTH, DON'T YOU?

TWO DAYS AGO, YOU CLAIMED YOU COULDN'T HAND IN YOUR ART HOMEWORK BECAUSE A GOAT HAD EATEN IT.

A GOAT? IN GLASGOW?

IT'S THE TRUTH!

I WAS IN THE COUNTRY FOR THE WEEKEND, AND A GOAT REALLY ATE MY DRAWING!

HMM.

AFTER THE SUMMER HOLIDAYS, I WILL ARRANGE A SESSION WITH THE SCHOOL COUNSELOR.

I WANT TO HELP YOU, CHERRY. NOT JUST WITH THE COMPULSIVE LYING, BUT WITH YOUR ANGER ISSUES.

I WON'T BE HERE AFTER THE SUMMER HOLIDAYS, MISS JARDINE. MY DAD HAS FALLEN IN LOVE.

WE'RE GOING TO LIVE WITH HIS GIRLFRIEND IN SOMERSET.

IN A BIG HOUSE ON THE EDGE OF A CLIFF!

McBEAN'S CHOCOLATE FACTORY HAS STOPPED MAKING CHOCOLATE TAYSTEE BARS, SO DAD'S LEAVING HIS JOB. HE'S GOING TO MAKE ORGANIC CHOCOLATES!

BYE, BYE, GLASGOW!

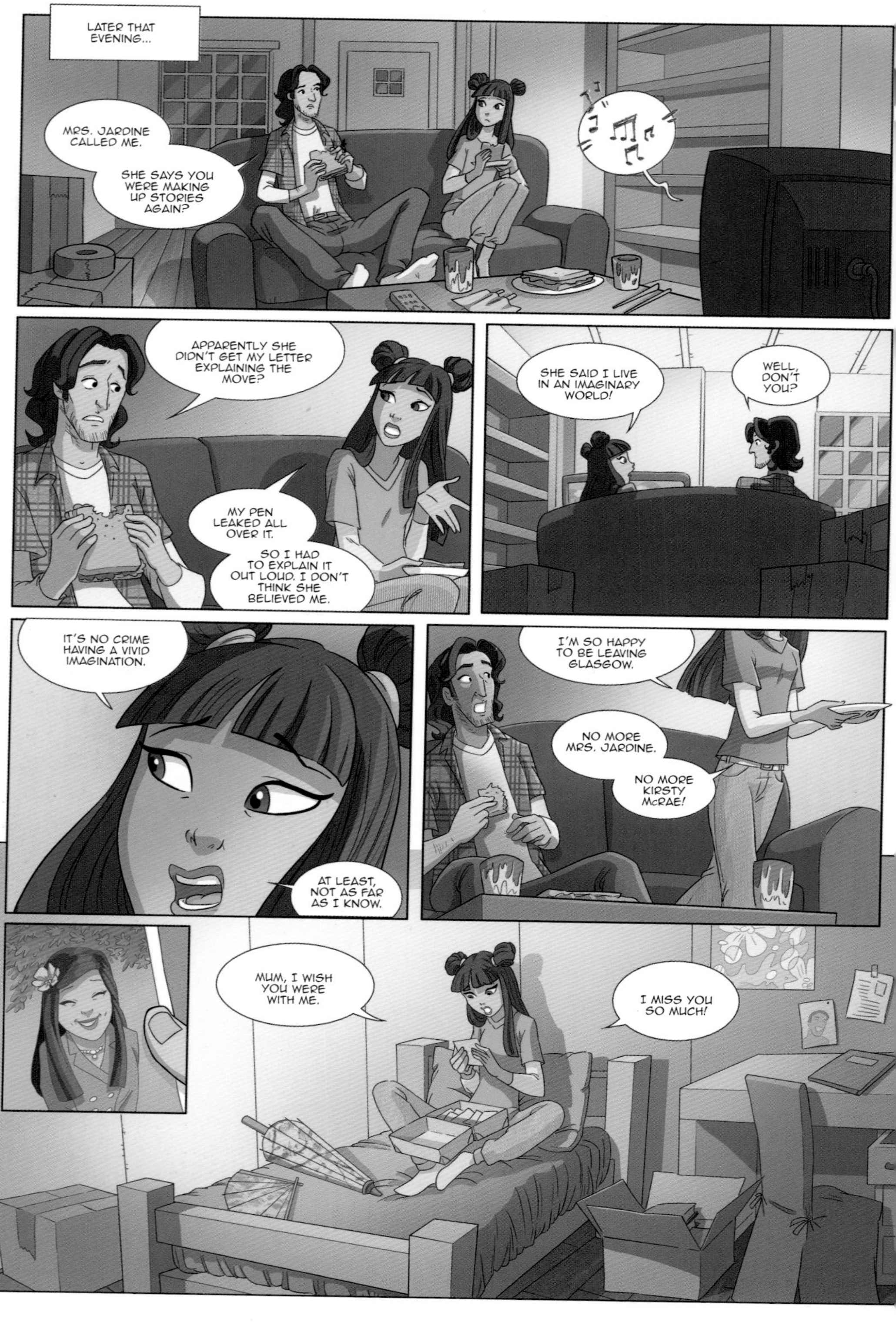
LATER THAT EVENING...
MRS. JARDINE CALLED ME.
SHE SAYS YOU WERE MAKING UP STORIES AGAIN?
APPARENTLY SHE DIDN'T GET MY LETTER EXPLAINING THE MOVE?
MY PEN LEAKED ALL OVER IT.
SO I HAD TO EXPLAIN IT OUT LOUD. I DON'T THINK SHE BELIEVED ME.
SHE SAID I LIVE IN AN IMAGINARY WORLD!
WELL, DON'T YOU?
IT'S NO CRIME HAVING A VIVID IMAGINATION.
AT LEAST, NOT AS FAR AS I KNOW.
I'M SO HAPPY TO BE LEAVING GLASGOW.
NO MORE MRS. JARDINE.
NO MORE KIRSTY McRAE!
MUM, I WISH YOU WERE WITH ME.
I MISS YOU SO MUCH!

I'VE ALWAYS WONDERED IF DAD MIGHT FIND SOMEONE NEW.

I DREAMED UP A HUNDRED DIFFERENT VERSIONS OF THE WOMAN WHO MIGHT BE MY NEW MUM...

...BUT I NEVER THOUGHT SHE'D ALREADY HAVE FOUR DAUGHTERS!

THE MORNING OF THE DEPARTURE...

I WON'T MISS THE RAIN!

I'LL MISS YOU, YOU KNOW!

YOU'RE THE NICEST NEIGHBOR, MRS. MACKIE!

PADDY...

...HOW DID YOU MEET YOUR CHARLOTTE?

THANKS TO AN INTERNET SITE WHERE YOU CAN CATCH UP WITH LONG-LOST FRIENDS.

TURNS OUT WE WERE STUDENTS AT ART-SCHOOL TOGETHER.

AMAZING, HUH?

CHARLOTTE'S BEEN DIVORCED FOR THREE YEARS AND OPENED A BED & BREAKFAST IN SOMERSET, ENGLAND.

SHE'S COOL.

SHE'S ALREADY BEEN HERE ONCE.

DOWN IN SOMERSET, DAD CAN GET HIS BUSINESS GOING!

THIS SUMMER-- WILL BE SORT OF A TRIAL RUN.

TO SEE WHETHER WE CAN MAKE THINGS WORK.

IF YOU'RE NOT HAPPY THERE, WE'LL COME BACK HERE.

YOU'RE STILL MY NUMBER-ONE GIRL, CHERRY. YOU KNOW THAT.

ALL RIGHT, IT'S TIME TO GO!

WILL YOU WRITE TO ME?

YES, MRS. MACKIE!

SKYE, SUMMER, AND COCO EACH WROTE ME A LETTER.

ONLY HONEY DIDN'T.

CHARLOTTE SAYS HONEY DIDN'T HAVE TIME TO WRITE A LETTER.

SHE'S THE ELDEST, SIX MONTHS OLDER THAN YOU.

YOU'LL BOTH BE IN THE SAME HIGH SCHOOL AFTER THE HOLIDAYS!

SHE'S VERY PRETTY, AND CLEVER, AND CONFIDENT...

I'M SURE YOU'LL BE GREAT FRIENDS!

I'M NOT PRETTY, OR CLEVER, OR CONFIDENT...

LIKE CHARLOTTE'S DAUGHTERS!

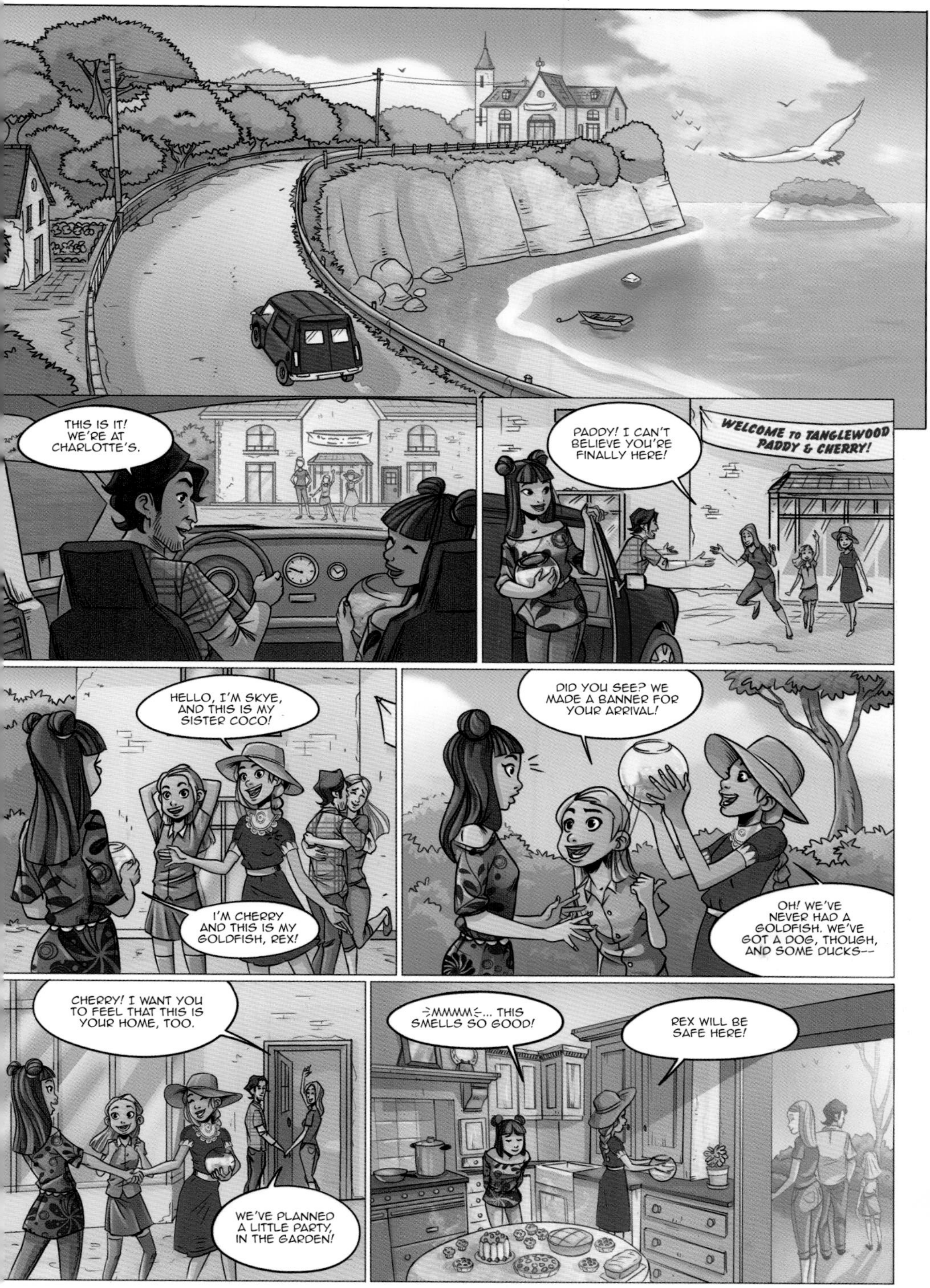
THIS IS IT! WE'RE AT CHARLOTTE'S.
PADDY! I CAN'T BELIEVE YOU'RE FINALLY HERE!
WELCOME TO TANGLEWOOD PADDY & CHERRY!
HELLO, I'M SKYE, AND THIS IS MY SISTER COCO!
I'M CHERRY AND THIS IS MY GOLDFISH, REX!
DID YOU SEE? WE MADE A BANNER FOR YOUR ARRIVAL!
OH! WE'VE NEVER HAD A GOLDFISH. WE'VE GOT A DOG, THOUGH, AND SOME DUCKS--
CHERRY! I WANT YOU TO FEEL THAT THIS IS YOUR HOME, TOO.
WE'VE PLANNED A LITTLE PARTY, IN THE GARDEN!
MMMM... THIS SMELLS SO GOOD!
REX WILL BE SAFE HERE!

ALL THESE CUPCAKES ARE SO BEAUTIFUL!

WE MADE THIS FOR YOU, ESPECIALLY... IT'S CHERRY CHOCOLATE COLA CAKE!

THANK YOU! IT SOUNDS-- UM--

AMAZING!

OH! A CARAVAN! IT'S SO BEAUTIFUL!

WE USED IT AS A CLUBHOUSE, WHEN WE WERE LITTLE!

HEY, HEY!

WHOA, THERE!

WOOF WOOF

OH, NO! I DROPPED EVERYTHING!

ARE YOU OKAY?

UH--YES, I THINK SO!

12

YOU'VE GOT TO BE CHERRY, RIGHT?

I'M SHAY FLETCHER!

SHAY—

HMMM, HE SMELLS OF WOOD SMOKE.

MAKE SURE HE DOESN'T EAT ANY CHOCOLATE!

RIGHT! WE DON'T WANT FRED TO GET SICK OR WORSE!

I'LL GO WITH YOU TO THE KITCHEN.

I SAID I'D GO GET SOME LOGS FOR THE BONFIRE!

RIGHT. SO, YOU ARE—?

ME? I'M NOBODY.

I'M NOT FAMILY OR ANYTHING, IF THAT'S WHAT YOU MEAN.

I LIVE DOWN IN THE VILLAGE AND GO TO HIGH SCHOOL WITH HONEY...

AND YOU, TOO, NOW, ACCORDING TO CHARLOTTE!

YOU'RE NOT A BIT LIKE I IMAGINED.

I'VE MET PADDY BEFORE, THE LAST TIME HE WAS DOWN, AND I THOUGHT YOU'D LOOK LIKE HIM—

I DON'T LOOK ANYTHING LIKE HIM. MY MUM WAS JAPANESE!

WOW! COOL!

NOT REALLY.

SHE HASN'T BEEN AROUND FOR A WHILE.

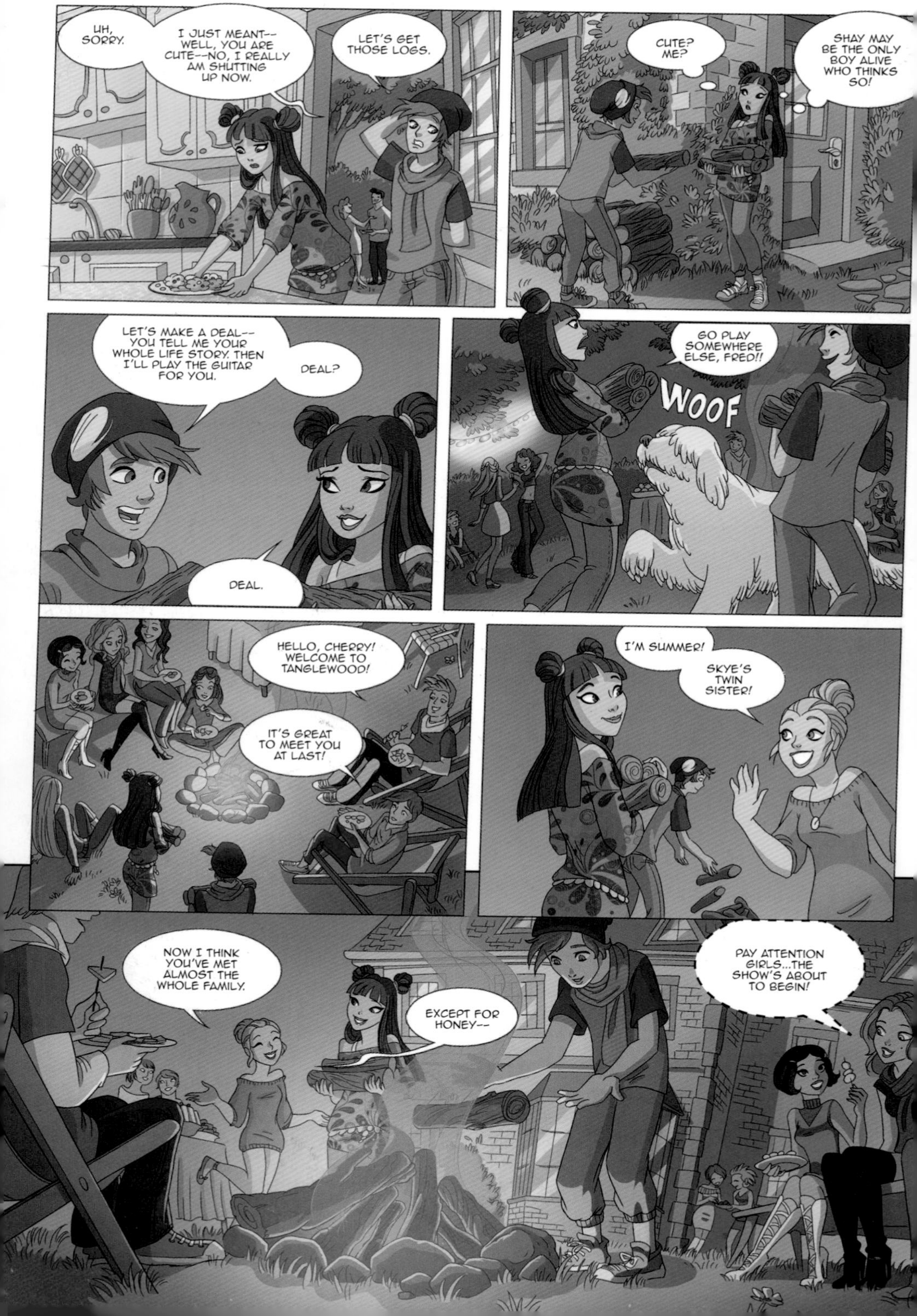
UH, SORRY.
I JUST MEANT-- WELL, YOU ARE CUTE--NO, I REALLY AM SHUTTING UP NOW.
LET'S GET THOSE LOGS.
CUTE? ME?
SHAY MAY BE THE ONLY BOY ALIVE WHO THINKS SO!
LET'S MAKE A DEAL-- YOU TELL ME YOUR WHOLE LIFE STORY. THEN I'LL PLAY THE GUITAR FOR YOU.
DEAL?
DEAL.
GO PLAY SOMEWHERE ELSE, FRED!!
WOOF
HELLO, CHERRY! WELCOME TO TANGLEWOOD!
IT'S GREAT TO MEET YOU AT LAST!
I'M SUMMER!
SKYE'S TWIN SISTER!
NOW I THINK YOU'VE MET ALMOST THE WHOLE FAMILY.
EXCEPT FOR HONEY--
PAY ATTENTION GIRLS...THE SHOW'S ABOUT TO BEGIN!

HEEHEEHEE HEEHEEHEE

THERE! NOW WE'RE **LOGGED**-IN TO THIS PARTY!

I FEEL LIKE A SORE THUMB BESIDE HONEY. SHE REMINDS ME OF KIRSTY McRAE.

I'M NOT HOME FREE YET!

DON'T YOU GET IT? "LOGGED-IN"?

I'M HONEY!

HI!

YOU'VE MET SHAY, THEN? MY BOYFRIEND?

UH—

LOOKS LIKE IT!

UH... LATER!

OOPS!

SHAY IS HONEY'S BOYFRIEND.

THE NEXT MORNING...

ONCE I MET HONEY, SHAY TURNED AWAY FROM ME AS IF I DIDN'T EXIST.

WHAT'S MORE, I GUESS I'M SHARING THE TURRET ROOM WITH THE PRINCESS. UGH.

DON'T YOU EVER KNOCK?

SHE'S--

SHE'S WEARING MY KIMONO!

DON'T YOU EVER THINK OF ASKING BEFORE YOU TAKE OTHER PEOPLE'S THINGS?!

THIS IS MY ROOM!

IF YOU LEAVE STUFF LYING AROUND, WHAT DO YOU EXPECT?

I DIDN'T LEAVE IT LYING AROUND, YOU WENT THROUGH MY STUFF!

YOU'RE THE ONE DIGGING INTO OTHER PEOPLE'S LIVES!

SHAY TOLD ME YOU WERE FLIRTING WITH HIM LAST NIGHT!

I MEAN, SERIOUSLY-- DON'T GO THERE, CHERRY!

HE'S OUT OF YOUR LEAGUE!

YOU THINK YOU'RE SO CLEVER.

YOU AND YOUR LOSER DAD. ONE MINUTE YOU'RE STUCK IN A GLASGOW SLUM! EATING REJECT CHOCOLATE BARS.

AND NOW YOU'RE INVADING MY SPACE!

LOSER DAD? IF THERE WAS A PLATE OF MACARONI HANDY RIGHT NOW--HONEY WOULD BE WEARING IT.

MY DAD HAD A GOOD JOB.

YEAH, RIGHT. SO, WHAT'S HE DOING HERE?

DAD'S GOING TO HELP CHARLOTTE WITH THE B&B!

AND THEY'RE GOING INTO BUSINESS MAKING HANDMADE, LUXURY CHOCOLATES!

USING WHOSE CASH?

MUM'S! SINCE YOUR DAD HASN'T A PENNY TO HIS NAME!

YOU AND YOUR DAD MAY HAVE FOOLED MY MUM AND MY SISTERS--

BUT YOU DON'T FOOL ME!

JUST LISTEN, OKAY? I DON'T WANT ANOTHER SISTER OR A NEW DAD.

I ALREADY HAVE A DAD.

HE'S SMART AND COOL AND HE LOVES ME!

WHAT'S YOUR PROBLEM?

WHAT HAVE I EVER DONE TO YOU?

GET OUT, CHERRY!

TAKE YOUR LAME STUFF AND JUST... GET OUT!

HEEEY!

HONEY? CHERRY? WHAT'S GOING ON?

HONEY? DOES THIS HAVE SOMETHING TO DO WITH YOU?

AS IF!

COME DOWN HERE RIGHT NOW!

THE BOX MUST HAVE FALLEN OFF THE WINDOW SILL!

SNIF

SNIF

HAVE YOU TWO ARGUED? IS THERE SOMETHING GOING ON HERE?

WHEN YOU'RE SHARING A ROOM--

YOU HAVE TO RESPECT OTHER PEOPLE'S POSSESSIONS!

I'LL BUY YOU ANOTHER FRAME!

IT'S NOTHING, DAD.

I DON'T WANT TO SHARE MY ROOM!

HONEY'S A BIT... MOODY RIGHT NOW.

IT'S BEST TO IGNORE HER.

18

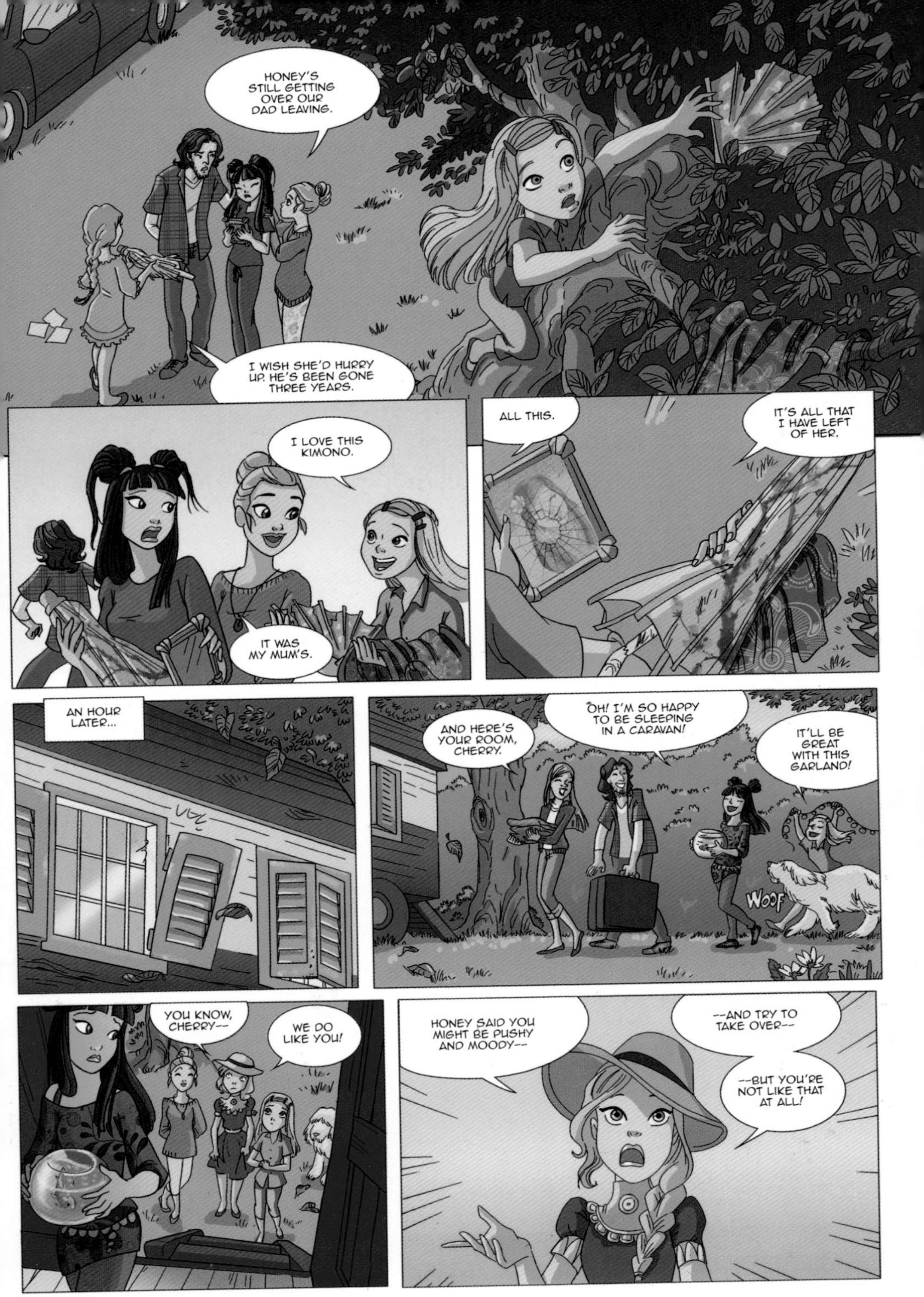
HONEY'S STILL GETTING OVER OUR DAD LEAVING.
I WISH SHE'D HURRY UP. HE'S BEEN GONE THREE YEARS.
I LOVE THIS KIMONO.
IT WAS MY MUM'S.
ALL THIS.
IT'S ALL THAT I HAVE LEFT OF HER.
AN HOUR LATER...
AND HERE'S YOUR ROOM, CHERRY.
OH! I'M SO HAPPY TO BE SLEEPING IN A CARAVAN!
IT'LL BE GREAT WITH THIS GARLAND!
WOOF
YOU KNOW, CHERRY--
WE DO LIKE YOU!
HONEY SAID YOU MIGHT BE PUSHY AND MOODY--
--AND TRY TO TAKE OVER--
--BUT YOU'RE NOT LIKE THAT AT ALL!

THE NEXT MORNING.

WOOF WOOF

ROOM SERVICE! BREAKFAST!

WOOF

DID YOU SLEEP OKAY, CHERRY?

YES, LIKE A BABY!

HOW ARE YOU?

I HAVEN'T HAD A CHANCE TO TALK TO YOU PROPERLY SINCE WE GOT HERE!

I'M OKAY! SKYE, SUMMER, AND COCO ARE REALLY NICE, AND CHARLOTTE IS LOVELY.

BUT--

I KNOW.

HONEY DOESN'T SEEM HAPPY THAT YOU AND I ARE HERE!

SHE'S NOT A HAPPY GIRL.

HONEY MIGHT TRY TO MAKE THINGS DIFFICULT.

TRY TO REMEMBER SHE'S NOT QUITE AS TOUGH AS SHE SEEMS!

IT'S NOT EASY TO BLEND TWO FAMILIES, BUT IT'S POSSIBLE--

AND I THINK IT'S WORTH THE EFFORT!

I KNOW!

WOOF

THE WEEK GOES BY...

THIS IS YOUR VACATION JOB, CHERRY-- HELPING US CLEAN THE B&B ROOMS.

TOMORROW IT'S YOUR TURN TO DO THE DUSTING!

AFTER ALL THAT EFFORT, IT'S CHILL TIME!

WHY DOESN'T HONEY EVER COME WITH US?

MOSTLY SHE STAYS IN HER ROOM.

SOMETIMES SHE GOES TO SEE FRIENDS!

CHERRY--

DO YOU WANT TO HAVE A TOUR OF THE VILLAGE?

OH! YES!

WELL GRAB YOUR BATHING SUIT AND LET'S GO!

YOU'LL SEE--

IT'S A REAL TOURIST TOWN!

THAT'S THE BOOKSTORE. THAT'S THE HARDWARE STORE.

AND THAT'S THE POST OFFICE.

Kitnor

IF YOU WANT TO GET SOME POSTCARDS FOR YOUR FRIENDS--

UH... YES... I'VE BEEN MEANING TO DO THAT!

THAT'S IT!

YOU MUST HAVE LOTS OF FRIENDS IN GLASGOW.

APART FROM MISS MACKIE-- NOT REALLY!

YES, TONS!

HELLO, SKYE!

ENJOYING THE SCHOOL HOLIDAYS?

YES! MRS. LEE, THIS IS CHERRY.

MY NEW STEPSISTER!

MRS. LEE HAS GYPSY BLOOD AND A SPECIAL GIFT. SHE CAN SEE THINGS.

"SEE" THINGS?

SENSE THINGS. I CAN SEE BENEATH THE SURFACE, TO THE TRUTH OF THINGS.

GIVE ME YOUR HAND!

I SEE--

A NEW FAMILY, TRUTH AND LIES--

DIFFICULT CHOICES--

WANT A MILKSHAKE?

The Mad Hatter~

OK!

GLI GLING

HEY, SKYE, CHERRY!

OVER HERE!

YOU CAN HAVE OUR SEATS. WE WERE JUST GOING!

WE WERE?

WE WERE!

I'M NOT HANGING AROUND HERE TO TALK DOLLS AND PONIES WITH MY LITTLE SISTER AND HER FREAKY FRIEND––

HONESTLY, HONEY––

LIKE WE'D WANT TO HANG OUT WITH YOU?

SHE WAS MEANT TO BE GOING UP TO LONDON THIS WEEKEND, TO SEE DAD...

...ONLY HE RANG LAST NIGHT AND CANCELLED IT.

SO HONEY'S EXTRA PRICKLY, RIGHT NOW.

DAD'S USELESS, ONLY SHE CAN'T SEE THAT.

OH? I'M SORRY!

I DON'T KNOW WHERE SHAY GETS THE PATIENCE!

I CAN'T STAND HER ANYMORE!

BUT I THINK SHE REALLY LOVES SHAY.

I DON'T THINK I LIKE HIM!

I CAN'T TELL HER I HAVE A CRUSH ON HIM!

WHAT?

YOU DON'T LIKE SHAY?

BUT EVERYONE LIKES HIM!

HE'S GREAT!

IT'S LIKE HE'S SOME KIND OF ADOPTED BROTHER—

YOU'LL LIKE HIM, ONCE YOU GET TO KNOW HIM.

I DON'T THINK SO.

I DON'T LIKE THE KIND OF BOY WHO, UHM... WEARS A HAT IN THE SUMMER...

OR WALKS AROUND WITH A GUITAR ACTING LIKE A ROCK STAR!

WHY DON'T I EVER TELL THE TRUTH?

SHAY LIVES THERE!

HIS DAD RUNS THE SAILING CENTER.

SHAY GIVES CLASSES TO THE GROCKLES DURING THE HOLIDAYS!

"GROCKLES?"

TOURISTS! IT'S WHAT WE CALL THEM DOWN HERE.

SAILING CENTRE

WANT TO SWIM?

I THOUGHT YOU'D NEVER AKS!

IT'S FANTASTIC!

COME IN!

BRRRR! IT'S LIKE THE ARCTIC OCEAN!

LET'S GO HOME ON THE BEACH, IT'S NICER!

I'LL SHOW YOU THE SMUGGLER'S CAVE!

Kitnor

Dear Mrs Mackie,
Settling in well. The house is beautiful and we are right by the beach, so I can swim whenever I want to. I am sleeping in a real cool gypsy caravan, along with Rex and a dog called Fred. Everyone is really nice

WELL...

...ALMOST EVERYONE!

≳MMM,≲ THAT SMELLS GOOD!

WHAT'S HONEY DOING?

WAIT, I'LL HELP YOU SET THE TABLE!

SHE'S IN HER ROOM.

SHE'S TURNING INTO A HERMIT, LATELY.

KLINK

HONEY!

WE'LL START WITHOUT HER.

IF WE WAIT FOR HER, IT'LL GO COLD.

ARE YOU OKAY?

IT'S MAKE-UP, OBVIOUSLY.

LOOKS LIKE HALLOWEEN'S COME EARLY.

I'M GOING TO GEORGIA'S.

WE'RE GOING TO WATCH TWILIGHT. I'LL EAT THERE!

YOU DON'T WANT MUM'S PASTA AND GARLIC--

--BECAUSE YOU'RE GOING TO KISS SHAY! HA HA!

PFFFT

AROUND MIDNIGHT...

NOK NOK

GRRR

?

NOK NOK

WHAT IF IT'S AN AXE-MURDERER?

CHERRY!

SHAY?

DID I SCARE YOU?

A BIT, YES.

PUT THE MASK BACK ON, QUICK!

GRRR

HA! VERY FUNNY!

UH...

I WAS JUST PASSING BY AND I THOUGHT I'D SAY HI.

WHAT ARE YOU DOING HERE?

DOES HONEY KNOW YOU'RE HERE?

UH---

I JUST WANTED TO SEE A FRIEND.

OKAY?

YOU WERE GOING TO TELL ME THE STORY OF YOUR LIFE.

AND IN EXCHANGE, YOU'LL PLAY THE GUITAR FOR ME?

THAT'S OUR DEAL!

ONCE UPON A TIME THERE WAS A YOUNG MAN NAMED PADDY--

--WHO WANTED TO PAINT THE WORLD WITH RAINBOW COLORS.

WHEN HE LEFT ART SCHOOL--

--HE WENT TRAVELING--

--AND MET A BEAUTIFUL JAPANESE GIRL NAMED KIKO.

THEY FELL IN LOVE--

--AND TRAVELED THE WORLD.

WHERE DO YOU COME IN?

I'M GETTING TO THAT BIT!

THEY SETTLED DOWN IN KYOTO AND HAD A BABY THEY NAMED SAKURA.

WHO IS THIS SAKURA PERSON?

HUSH!

SAKURA MEANS CHERRY BLOSSOM!

ONE MORNING, ALL THREE OF THEM WENT TO THE TEMPLE. IT WAS THE DAY THE CHERRIES WERE BLOOMING.

THE DAY WHEN THE CHERRIES LOSE THEIR FLOWERS--

AND FLY OFF IN THE WIND--

SAKURA DISCOVERED HER MUM HAD DISAPPEARED.

OHHH!

IT'S GETTING LATE. YOU HAVE TO GO NOW--IT'S GETTING LATE.

YOU CAN PLAY FOR ME ANOTHER TIME.

BUT THE REST OF THE STORY?!

WHAT HAPPENED TO SAKURA'S MUM?

JUST GO, OKAY?

PLEASE.

WOOF

YOU SHOULDN'T EVEN BE HERE.

THE NEXT MORNING...

REX, SHAY FLETCHER IS BAD NEWS!

HE IS OFF-LIMITS!

HE BELONGS TO SOMEONE ELSE.

SOMEONE WHO HATES ME.

YOU'RE TALKING TO A GOLDFISH?

YES, BUT THE ONLY PROBLEM IS, WHEN YOU CONFIDE IN A FISH--

--THERE'S NO DISCUSSION!

YOUR REX NEEDS MORE ROOM!

WE COULD DIG A FISHPOND!

WHO'S COMING TO THE BEACH?

FIRST ONE HOME GETS ICE CREAM!

OOOOOH!

IT LOOKS LIKE IT'S BEEN BURGLED--

AND RANSACKED BY VANDALS!

KLING KLONG

AH! YOU'RE JUST IN TIME!

YOU'LL GET TO TASTE MY CREATIONS!

KLING KLING

I MADE CURRY TRUFFLES--

LOVELY, UM--

HOW OFTEN ARE YOU PLANNING ON DOING THIS?

HMMMM, THISH ISH GOOD!

I'M NOT SURE MY NERVES CAN TAKE IT!

I KNOW THE KITCHEN TABLE ISN'T THE BEST PLACE FOR A CHOCOLATE BUSINESS!

HMMMM, I LOVE THE CURRY CHOCOLATE!

OK, GIRLS--

FAMILY MEETING!

BUT BEFORE STUFFING YOURSELVES ON CHOCOLATES--

DISHES!

WHAT'S ALL THIS MESS?

YOU WANT TO TASTE PADDY'S TRUFFLES?

I DON'T LIKE CHOCOLATE!

ANYWAY, WE'RE ALL HERE--

I THOUGHT WE COULD DISCUSS THE CHOCOLATE BUSINESS!

THE PROCESS FOR MAKING CHOCOLATE IS LONG. THE BEST COCOA BEANS MUST BE SELECTED.

I'LL INVEST IN A GAS GRILL, A ROASTING DRUM--

OH! YEAH--

AND WHERE'S THE MONEY GOING TO COME FROM?

YOU THINK YOU CAN USE MUM'S MONEY TO FINANCE IT ALL?

HONEY! STOP THAT RIGHT NOW! PADDY HAS SAVINGS--

I WON'T HAVE THAT KIND OF TALK HERE!

WELL, HE BETTER NOT PUT HIS GROSS FACTORY IN THE GARAGE. THAT'S WHERE DAD PUT HIS VINTAGE CARS!

SO, DON'T GO THERE!

HONEY! APOLOGIZE TO PADDY RIGHT NOW!

APOLOGIZE? NO WAY!

YOU'RE NOT MY DAD!

DING

OOOH!

KLONG

KLONK

I--

I DIDN'T MEAN TO UPSET HONEY!

SLAM

EVERYTHING SEEMS TO UPSET HER, LATELY. I DON'T KNOW WHAT TO DO ANYMORE!

SHE NEEDS TO SPEND THE WEEKEND WITH HER FATHER. THE TWO OF THEM NEED TO TALK!

STAYING FOR DINNER, SHAY?

OKAY, THANKS!

SO, WHAT'S THIS CHOCOLATE BUSINESS--

--GOING TO BE CALLED?

GOOD QUESTION!

HOW ABOUT "KITNOR CHOCOLATES"?

"TANGLEWOOD TRUFFLES"?

WHAT IF YOU CALLED IT: "THE CHOCOLATE BOX"?

IN BEAUTIFUL, LITTLE BOXES TIED UP WITH A RIBBON!

YEAH, THAT'S GREAT!

HMMMM, I LIKE THAT!

I HAVE AN IDEA!

YOU'LL SIGN UP FOR THE FOOD FESTIVAL THAT'S TAKING PLACE IN A FEW WEEKS, IT'LL BE A TEST!

UH--

SOUNDS GOOD!

BUT I'LL NEED SOME HELPFUL CHOCOLATE FAIRIES WITH ME!

33

LATER THAT EVENING...

SHAY!

WHAT ARE YOU DOING?

I WAS WAITING FOR YOU!

YOU DIDN'T FINISH TELLING ME THE STORY OF SAKURA.

AFTERWARDS, I'LL PLAY THE GUITAR FOR YOU!

OKAY--

BUT TELL ME ABOUT YOU, FIRST!

TRUST ME, YOU DON'T WANT TO KNOW. MY DAD HATES ME, AND MY GIRLFRIEND IS TURNING INTO A PSYCHO!

I--

I LIKE YOU. YOU KNOW--

I CAN'T HELP IT.

ME, TOO! YOU'RE DIFFERENT--

INTERESTING!

TELL ME ABOUT SAKURA.

PLEASE!

SAKURA DIDN'T UNDERSTAND WHY HER MOTHER HAD DISAPPEARED—

SHE MISSED HER.

SHE OFTEN ASKED ABOUT HER.

SHE WANTED TO KNOW WHERE SHE'D GONE AND WHEN SHE MIGHT BE COMING HOME.

SAKURA'S DAD NEVER ANSWERED HER QUESTIONS, BUT JUST HUGGED HER CLOSE.

A FEW MONTHS LATER, HE GAVE HER A KIMONO SCENTED WITH HER MOTHER'S PERFUME!

ZZZz

THAT WAS THE KIMONO HONEY THREW OUT THE WINDOW. CHARLOTTE WASHED IT AND THE PERFUME DISAPPEARED, IS THAT IT?

YES!

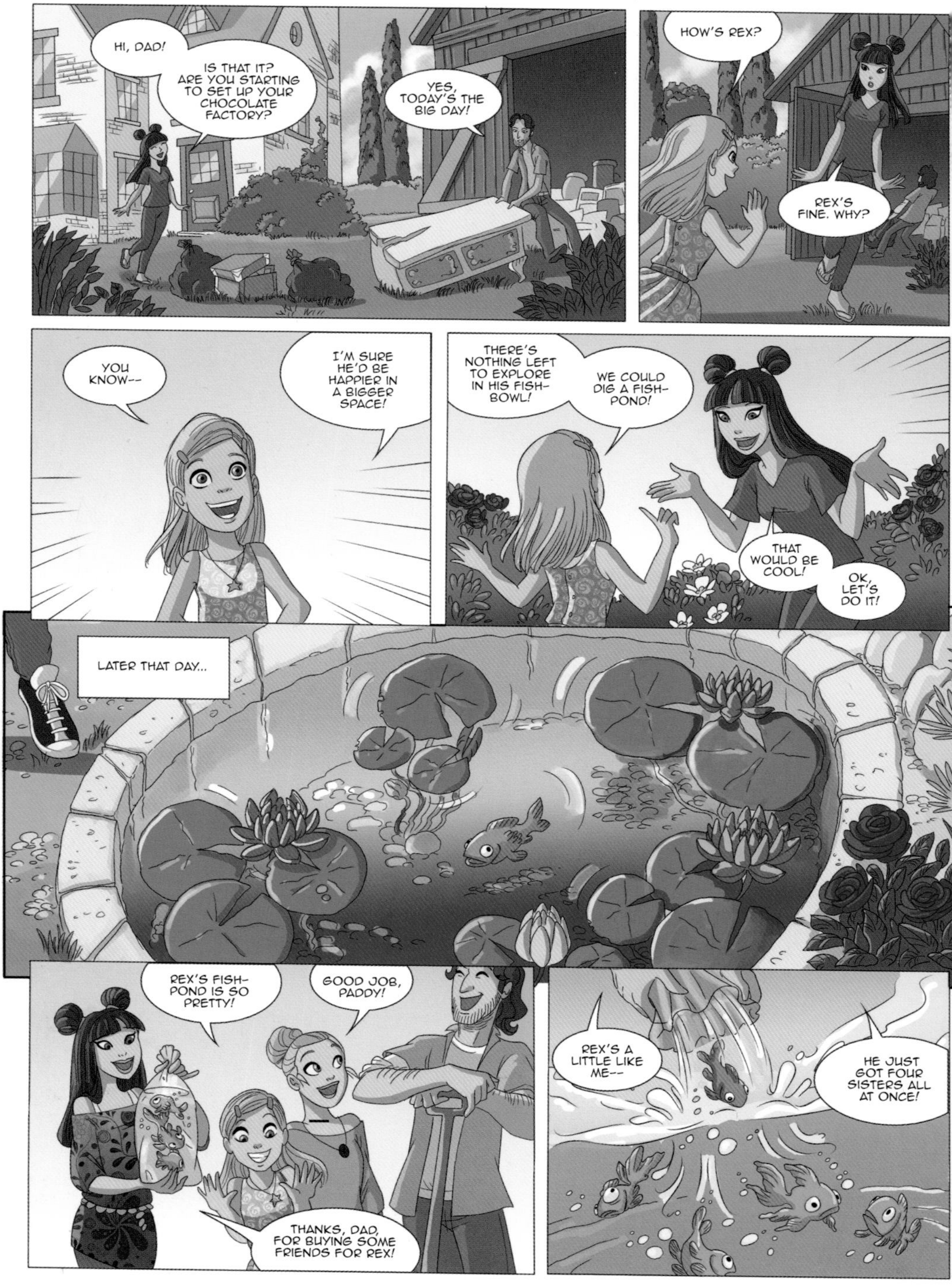
HI, DAD!
IS THAT IT? ARE YOU STARTING TO SET UP YOUR CHOCOLATE FACTORY?
YES, TODAY'S THE BIG DAY!
HOW'S REX?
REX'S FINE. WHY?
YOU KNOW--
I'M SURE HE'D BE HAPPIER IN A BIGGER SPACE!
THERE'S NOTHING LEFT TO EXPLORE IN HIS FISH-BOWL!
WE COULD DIG A FISH-POND!
THAT WOULD BE COOL!
OK, LET'S DO IT!
LATER THAT DAY...
REX'S FISH-POND IS SO PRETTY!
GOOD JOB, PADDY!
THANKS, DAD, FOR BUYING SOME FRIENDS FOR REX!
REX'S A LITTLE LIKE ME--
HE JUST GOT FOUR SISTERS ALL AT ONCE!

A FEW DAYS LATER...

WHAT ARE YOU DOING?

I'M SEEING IF REX LIKES HIS FISHPOND!

IT'S WEIRD CALLING YOUR FISH A DOG'S NAME!

I THINK IT'S FUNNY--

THAT'S ALL.

MOVE OVER--

I HAVE STUFF TO DO FOR MY ART PROJECT AND YOU'RE IN THE WAY!

I KNOW YOU DON'T LIKE ME, HONEY!

BUT YOU COULD MAKE AN EFFORT TO BE POLITE, COULDN'T YOU?

I CAN'T STAND YOU!

END OF STORY!

YOU'LL NEVER FIT IN HERE!

THIS WHOLE STEPFAMILY THING IS NOT GOING TO WORK!

YOU KNOW WHAT?

THE TRUTH IS, MY MUM'S USING PADDY TO MAKE DAD JEALOUS!

AND THERE'S REALLY NO POINT IN US BECOMING SISTERS!

THAT GIRL'S NOTHING BUT A POISONOUS VIPER!

PLOP

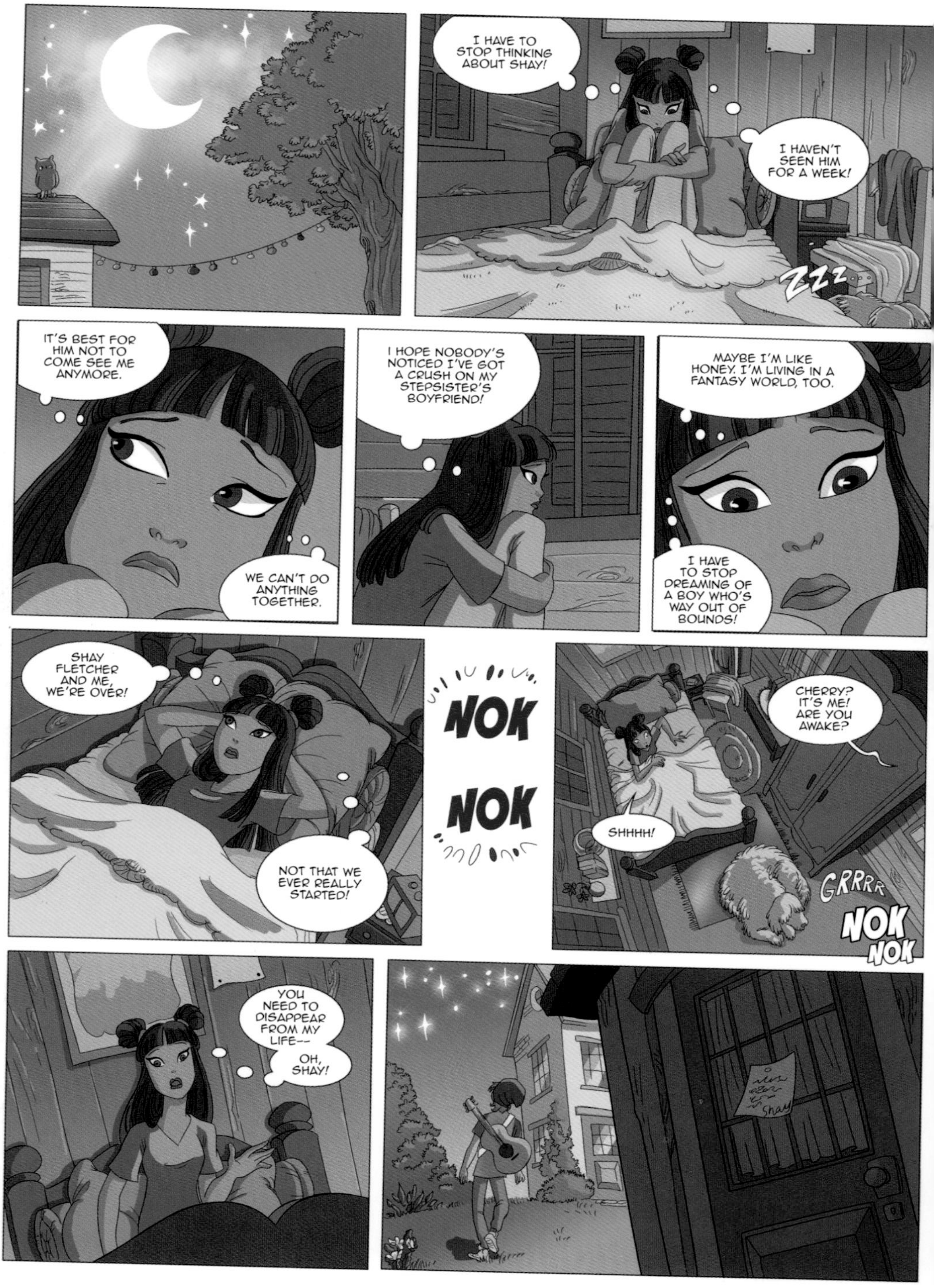
I HAVE TO STOP THINKING ABOUT SHAY!
I HAVEN'T SEEN HIM FOR A WEEK!
ZZZ
IT'S BEST FOR HIM NOT TO COME SEE ME ANYMORE.
WE CAN'T DO ANYTHING TOGETHER.
I HOPE NOBODY'S NOTICED I'VE GOT A CRUSH ON MY STEPSISTER'S BOYFRIEND!
MAYBE I'M LIKE HONEY. I'M LIVING IN A FANTASY WORLD, TOO.
I HAVE TO STOP DREAMING OF A BOY WHO'S WAY OUT OF BOUNDS!
SHAY FLETCHER AND ME, WE'RE OVER!
NOT THAT WE EVER REALLY STARTED!
NOK
NOK
CHERRY? IT'S ME! ARE YOU AWAKE?
SHHHH!
GRRRR
NOK
NOK
YOU NEED TO DISAPPEAR FROM MY LIFE--
OH, SHAY!
SHAY

*"HAIKU," A SHORT JAPANESE POEM.

US BEING FRIENDS--

IT'S NOT GOING TO WORK!

COME ON, SHAY! WE'VE GOT THINGS TO DO!

NO, FRED! LEAVE ME ALONE!

SMACK

I'M GOING TO HAVE BREAKFAST. BYE!

THAT AFTERNOON...

HEY!

WHAT ARE YOU DOING?

I'M TAKING MY GROCKLES TO THE SMUGGLERS' CAVE!

THAT BOY IS EVERYWHERE!

HIS CHARM DOESN'T WORK ON YOU?

≥PFFF!≤

NO!

WEIRD!

GIRLS ARE USUALLY ALL OVER HIM!

TEST ANSWER: THE BOY YOU'RE CRUSHING ON INVADES YOUR DREAMS, YOUR HEAD--

AND YOUR HEART--

YOU IMAGINE A MILLION DIFFERENT WAYS YOU CAN BE TOGETHER, BUT IT'S ALL FOR NOTHING, BECAUSE HE'S OUT OF REACH.

GIRL MAG

TO FORGET SOMEBODY, YOU HAVE TO KEEP BUSY!

LET'S GO HOME!

I WANT TO DO SOMETHING BESIDES CRAZY, MAGAZINE TESTS!

OKAY!

AT TANGLEWOOD HOUSE...

I GOT IT!

HE GOT WHAT?

HIS LOAN FOR THE CHOCOLATE FACTORY!

THAT'S GREAT!

AND SECOND BIT OF GOOD NEWS, WE'RE IN THE FOOD FESTIVAL!

AND THIRD BIT OF GOOD NEWS--

UH...

CHARLOTTE...

WILL YOU MARRY ME?

OH! PADDY!

OF COURSE, YES!

NO!

HOW CAN YOU, MUM?

YOU ALREADY HAVE A HUSBAND--

MY DAD!

YOU'RE NOT MY DAD, AND YOU NEVER WILL BE!

WE DON'T NEED YOU!

HONEY, CALM DOWN--

STOP IT, PLEASE!

YOU KNOW YOUR FATHER AND I ARE DIVORCED!

THIS ISN'T YOUR HOME, PADDY COSTELLO!

YOU WORMED YOUR WAY IN WITH YOUR LOSER DAUGHTER!

I HATE YOU BOTH!

I'M SORRY!

LET HER CALM DOWN!

SLAM

AFTER DINNER...

I HEARD THE MUSIC ON MY WAY BACK TO THE CARAVAN.

YOU OKAY?

NO! HONEY YELLED AT ME.

I'M SICK OF IT!

HONEY'S ONE MIXED-UP GIRL.

I'M NOT EVEN SURE WHAT I'M DOING WITH SOMEONE LIKE THAT.

YOU LOVE HER. SHE'S YOUR GIRLFRIEND!

I DON'T LOVE HER.

IT'S ALL ABOUT HER. SHE NEVER ASKS HOW STUFF IS GOING IN MY LIFE. MY DAD HATES ME--

MY DAD THINKS I'M USELESS!

I'M TIRED OF PUTTING UP WITH THIS!

WANT TO SWIM?

YEAH, COOL!

SPLASH

SPLASH

YOU HAVE TO MAKE A WISH WHEN YOU SWIM AT MIDNIGHT!

I WISH YOU WOULD FALL IN LOVE WITH ME!

LALALAAA!

IT'S LIKE HONEY HAS HAD A WHOLE PERSONALITY TRANSPLANT!

SHE'S IN A GOOD MOOD THIS MORNING!

SHE'S SPENDING NEXT WEEKEND WITH DAD.

IN LONDON, JUST THE TWO OF THEM! LET'S HOPE DAD DOESN'T CANCEL THIS TIME!

T-MINUS 3 DAYS BEFORE THE FOOD FESTIVAL!

GIRLS, TEST SESSION FOR NEW FLAVORS: STRAWBERRY SWIRL, MOCHA MELT, CHERRY CRUSH!

PADDY— YOUR TRUFFLES ARE AWESOME!

YUM!

I'M TASTING CHERRY CRUSH!

WE JUST GOT THE BOXES.

ASSEMBLY SESSION AFTER BREAKFAST!

AND AFTERWARDS—

FITTING SESSION FOR THE CHOCOLATE FAIRY COSTUMES!

FINALLY! THE DAY OF THE FOOD FESTIVAL...

SHAY!

YOU'RE SUPPOSED TO BE WORKING AT THE SAILING CENTER!

SHAY GAVE US A HAND WITH THE FOOD FESTIVAL!

YOUR SON'S A GREAT KID, YOU KNOW?

I DON'T LIKE HIM HANGING AROUND YOU!

HE'S GOT NOTHING TO DO AT YOUR BLOOMIN' FESTIVAL!

YOU GET HOME!

THE MAN'S A MONSTER!

THE CHOCOLAT

LATER, THAT DAY...

I'M WORN OUT--

"THE CHOCOLATE BOX" IS A HUGE SUCCESS!

SHAY JUST TEXTED ME. HE'S GROUNDED!

HE CAN'T GO OUT FOR THREE DAYS!

YEAH, WE'LL EVEN HAVE AN ARTICLE IN THE NEWSPAPER! COOL!

YOU DON'T CARE!

YOU'RE GOING TO LONDON TOMORROW!

HEY, THAT'S DAD, NOW!

BEEDEE BEEDEE BEEDEE

WHAT?

NOOOOO!

YOU CAN'T DO THIS TO ME!

ARE YOU OKAY?

WHAT DO YOU CARE, ANYHOW?

AND BING! DAD'S CANCELLED THE WEEKEND ONCE AGAIN!

YOU GET ON MY NERVES! YOU'RE NOTHING BUT A HYPOCRITE. YOU HAVE NO FRIENDS.

YOU HAVE A PATHETIC LIFE-- AND YOU TOLD US LIES!

YOU CAN'T SAY THAT!

YOU TOLD US YOU LIVED IN A BIG APARTMENT IN GLASGOW, THAT YOU HAD A BOYFRIEND, THAT YOUR DAD WAS RICH.

BUT NONE OF IT'S TRUE!

YOUR FATHER WAS WORKING ON A CHOCOLATE FACTORY PRODUCTION LINE!

SHE'S A LIAR, A CHEAT, AND A PHONY!

SHE'S TAKEN YOU ALL IN WITH HER STUPID STORIES!

SHE NEVER HAD ANY FRIENDS!

I--

I WANTED YOU TO ACCEPT ME!

SOMETIMES PEOPLE MIX UP THEIR DREAMS WITH REALITY.

CHERRY DIDN'T MEAN ANY HARM!

THAT'S RIGHT, DEFEND LITTLE MISS PERFECT!

SHE'S BEEN MANIPULATING YOU WITH HER STORIES, TOO!

WHEN YOU'D GO MEET HER AT NIGHT!

WHAT? IS THAT TRUE, CHERRY?

IT WASN'T LIKE THAT!

WE'RE JUST FRIENDS. WE LIKE TO TALK TO EACH OTHER, THAT'S ALL!

I DON'T WANT YOU!

SHAY FLETCHER, GET OUT OF MY LIFE!

AND YOU--

SLAP

I HATE YOU!

LEAVE ME ALONE!

I THOUGHT YOU WERE GROUNDED. WHAT ARE YOU DOING HERE?

I WANTED A FAMILY--

I'VE RUINED EVERYTHING!

HEY!

COME BACK!

DON'T CRY, COCO. IT'LL BE ALL RIGHT!

WHERE ARE YOU GOING?

I JUST WANT TO GO AWAY!

TO FIND A MAGICAL LAND WHERE NOBODY HATES ME!

SKYE, YOU ALL CAN GO HOME.

WE'RE JUST TAKING A SHORT TRIP!

ARE YOU TAKING ME TO THE SMUGGLERS' CAVE?

NO, WE'RE GOING BACK IN TEN MINUTES.

IT'S GETTING DARK! AND MY DAD MUST BE LOOKING EVERYWHERE FOR ME!

A HALF-HOUR LATER...

I CAN'T TELL WHERE WE ARE--

THE CURRENT HAS PULLED US FAR FROM THE SHORE!

AAAAAH!

A ROCK!

KKRAAAK

WE HAVE TO SWIM TOWARDS THE ROCKS!

I--

I--WON'T MAKE IT!

47

YOU WANTED TO SEE THE SMUGGLERS' CAVE--

WE MADE IT!

SHAY, I'M SORRY. THIS IS MY FAULT.

THE CANOE-- YOUR DAD--

IT'S OKAY. I'LL JUST BE GROUNDED FOR THE REST OF MY LIFE!

MY CELLPHONE IS DEAD, LOOKS LIKE WE'LL JUST HAVE TO WAIT!

MY DAD WILL BE WORRIED!

I'M COLD!

COME CLOSER TO ME.

AND TELL ME MORE ABOUT SAKURA!

I HAVE TO TELL YOU SOMETHING.

I MADE UP THAT STORY.

MY MUM DIED WHEN I WAS FOUR. I'VE NEVER LIVED IN JAPAN.

YOU KNOW, YOUR STORIES ARE REALLY BEAUTIFUL. YOU SHOULD WRITE THEM DOWN!

I LOVE BEING WITH YOU.

I'VE FELT THIS WAY EVER SINCE I FIRST SAW YOU!

I'LL TELL HONEY. I'LL EXPLAIN SO SHE DOESN'T BLAME YOU.

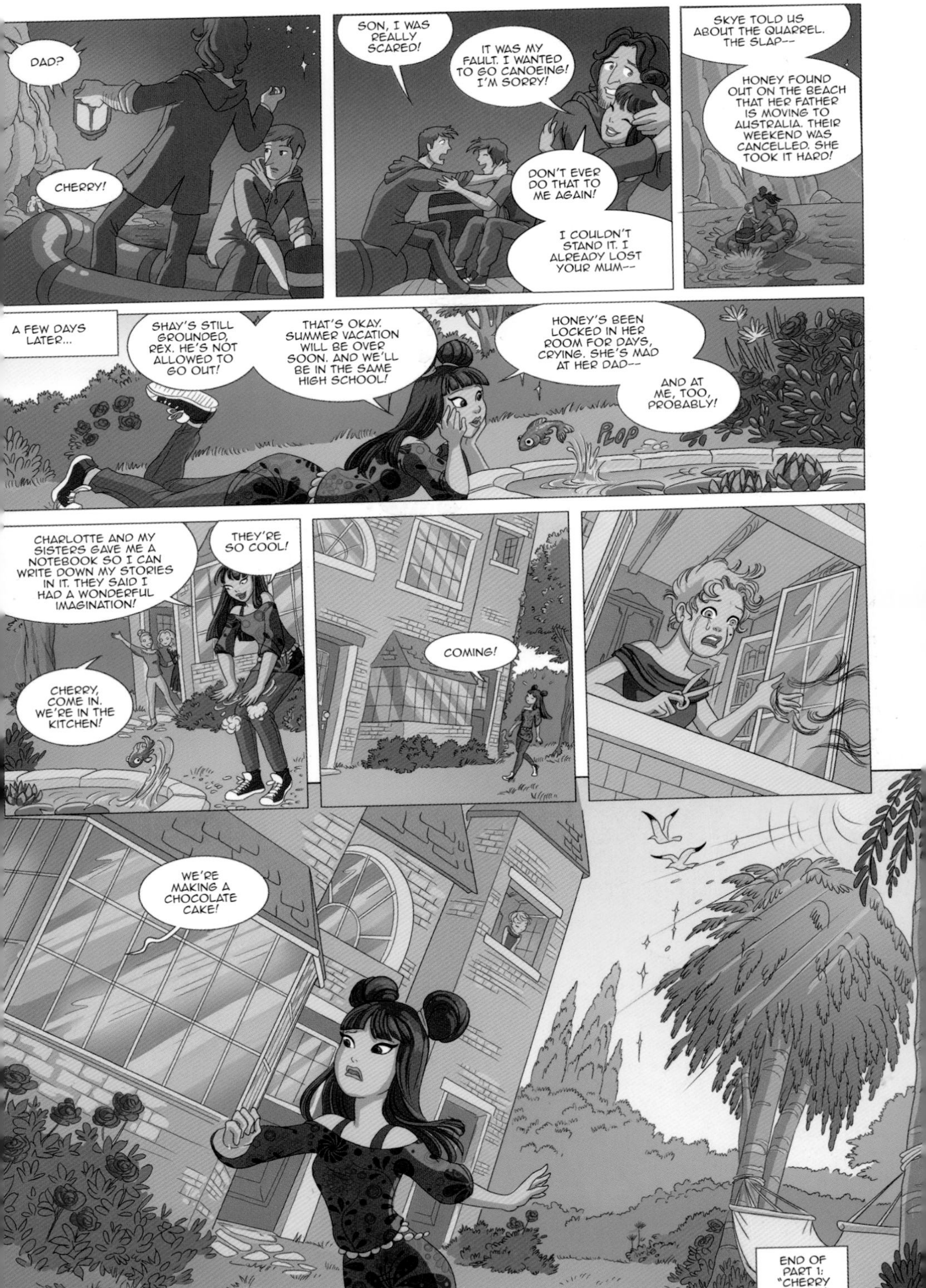
DAD?
CHERRY!
SON, I WAS REALLY SCARED!
IT WAS MY FAULT. I WANTED TO GO CANOEING! I'M SORRY!
DON'T EVER DO THAT TO ME AGAIN!
I COULDN'T STAND IT. I ALREADY LOST YOUR MUM--
SKYE TOLD US ABOUT THE QUARREL. THE SLAP--
HONEY FOUND OUT ON THE BEACH THAT HER FATHER IS MOVING TO AUSTRALIA. THEIR WEEKEND WAS CANCELLED. SHE TOOK IT HARD!
A FEW DAYS LATER...
SHAY'S STILL GROUNDED, REX. HE'S NOT ALLOWED TO GO OUT!
THAT'S OKAY. SUMMER VACATION WILL BE OVER SOON. AND WE'LL BE IN THE SAME HIGH SCHOOL!
HONEY'S BEEN LOCKED IN HER ROOM FOR DAYS, CRYING. SHE'S MAD AT HER DAD--
AND AT ME, TOO, PROBABLY!
PLOP
CHARLOTTE AND MY SISTERS GAVE ME A NOTEBOOK SO I CAN WRITE DOWN MY STORIES IN IT. THEY SAID I HAD A WONDERFUL IMAGINATION!
THEY'RE SO COOL!
CHERRY, COME IN. WE'RE IN THE KITCHEN!
COMING!
WE'RE MAKING A CHOCOLATE CAKE!
END OF PART 1: "CHERRY CRUSH."

I DON'T BELIEVE IN GHOSTS. I DO BELIEVE IN CREAKY FLOORBOARDS, IN HOWLING SOUNDS THROUGH THE EAVES, BECAUSE WHEN YOU LIVE IN A BIG, OLD HOUSE LIKE TANGLEWOOD, THOSE THINGS ARE PART OF THE DEAL.

DON'T YOU THINK OUR OUTFITS MATCH WITH TANGLEWOOD, SKYE?

YES! OUR HOUSE LOOKS A LITTLE LIKE IT COULD BE HAUNTED. I'VE NEVER SEEN ANY GHOSTS HERE--BESIDES US TWO TONIGHT!

THE ONLY GHOSTS I BELIEVE IN ARE THE HALLOWEEN VARIETY, SMALL AND STICKY-FACED AND DRESSED IN WHITE SHEETS, CLUTCHING A BAG OF CANDY.

SKYE! SUMMER--

HURRY UP! CHERRY'S DOWNSTAIRS WAITING. WE'LL MISS THE PARTY!

YOU MEAN LITTLE MONSTERS LIKE COCO!

HEE HEE!

COMING!

WE'RE NOT TWINS FOR NOTHING. WE SAY AND DO THINGS ALIKE-- WELL ALMOST!

SUMMER CAME INTO THE WORLD FIRST, A WHOLE FOUR MINUTES AHEAD OF ME, DAZZLING, DARING, DETERMINED TO SHINE. I FOLLOWED AFTER, PINK-FACED AND HOWLING.

IF SHE WAS SMILING, I SMILED, TOO. IF SHE WAS CRYING, I'D CRY, TOO.

WE BOTH WENT TO BALLET CLASS BACK THEN. SUMMER LOVED IT, IT WAS HER PASSION. I THOUGHT IT WAS MINE, TOO--

BUT REALLY I WAS JUST A MIRROR GIRL, REFLECTING MY TWIN.

COMING?

GO AHEAD, I'LL BE A MINUTE!

THE YEAR WHEN DAD LEFT MOM. I WAS FED UP WITH PRETENDING. I DIDN'T LOVE BALLET. I STOPPED. SUMMER DIDN'T UNDERSTAND THAT; FROM "US," I'D SHIFTED TO "YOU" AND "ME." IT WAS GOOD FOR ME!

???

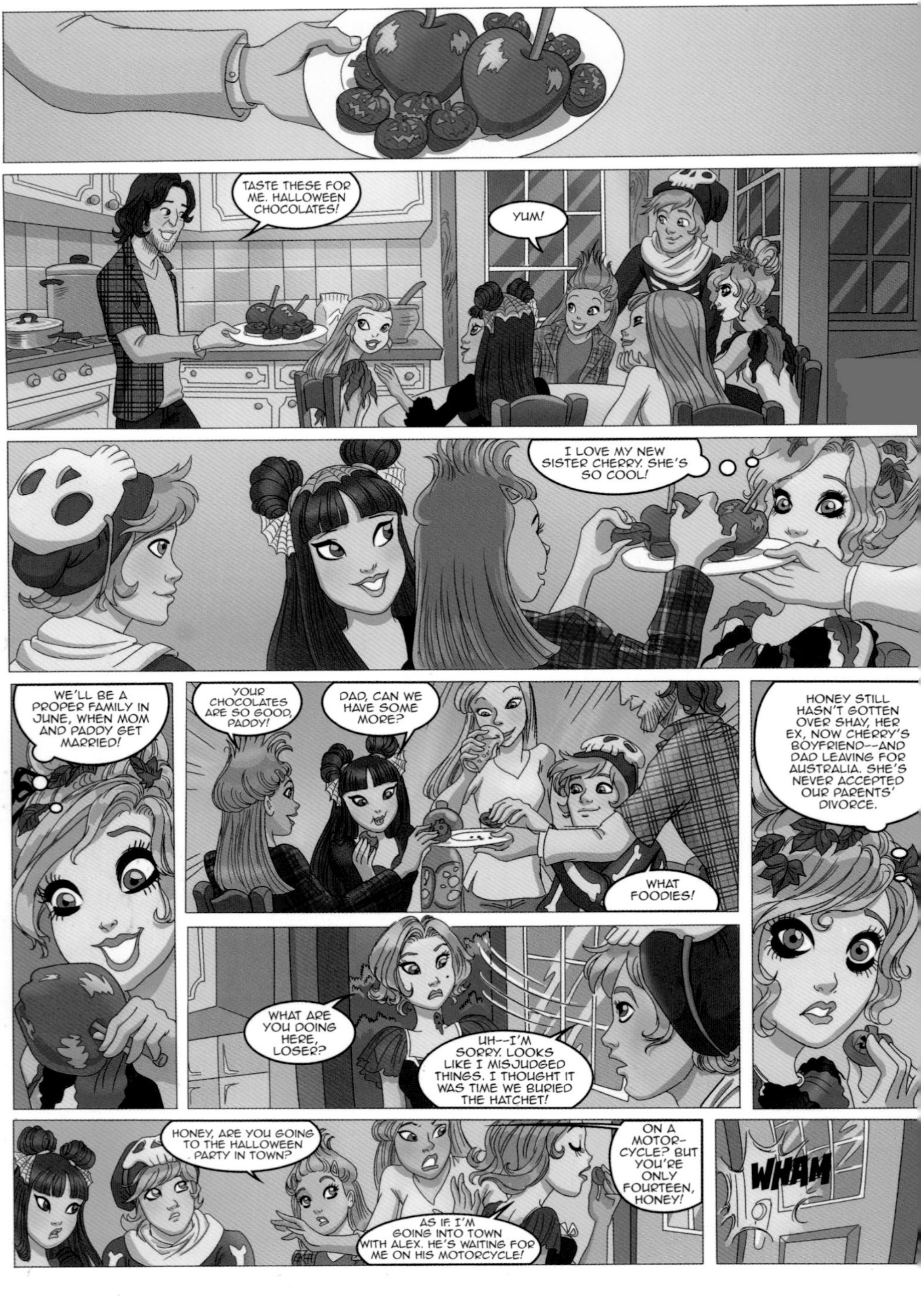
TASTE THESE FOR ME. HALLOWEEN CHOCOLATES!
YUM!
I LOVE MY NEW SISTER CHERRY. SHE'S SO COOL!
WE'LL BE A PROPER FAMILY IN JUNE, WHEN MOM AND PADDY GET MARRIED!
YOUR CHOCOLATES ARE SO GOOD, PADDY!
DAD, CAN WE HAVE SOME MORE?
WHAT FOODIES!
HONEY STILL HASN'T GOTTEN OVER SHAY, HER EX, NOW CHERRY'S BOYFRIEND--AND DAD LEAVING FOR AUSTRALIA. SHE'S NEVER ACCEPTED OUR PARENTS' DIVORCE.
WHAT ARE YOU DOING HERE, LOSER?
UH--I'M SORRY. LOOKS LIKE I MISJUDGED THINGS. I THOUGHT IT WAS TIME WE BURIED THE HATCHET!
HONEY, ARE YOU GOING TO THE HALLOWEEN PARTY IN TOWN?
AS IF. I'M GOING INTO TOWN WITH ALEX. HE'S WAITING FOR ME ON HIS MOTORCYCLE!
ON A MOTOR-CYCLE? BUT YOU'RE ONLY FOURTEEN, HONEY!
WHAM

THIS HALLOWEEN PARTY IS LAME! AVERAGE AGE: SIX-YEARS-OLD!

LET'S GO BACK TO THE CARAVAN. WE COULD TELL GHOST STORIES!

OH! YES! COOL!

SLOOPFFF! SLOOPFF!

DID YOU HEAR SOMETHING? LIKE-- WELL, GHOSTLY FOOTSTEPS?

GHOSTS DON'T HAVE FOOTSTEPS! THEY JUST GLIDE RIGHT THROUGH YOU, LIKE A COLD FINGER SLIDING DOWN YOUR SPINE!

YOU HAVE TOO MUCH IMAGINATION, CHERRY!

WE'RE HEADING HOME TO TELL GHOST STORIES!

I KNOW LOTS OF REALLY BLOODTHIRSTY ONES, CAN I COME?

BOOOOOOOOO!

AAAARGH!

EEEEEEE!

WHERE YA GOING?

WHO'S THE ZOMBIE?

ALFIE ANDERSON, A CHAMPION OF BAD PRACTICAL JOKES. HE GOES TO MIDDLE SCHOOL WITH US. WE'VE KNOWN HIM SINCE PRE-K.

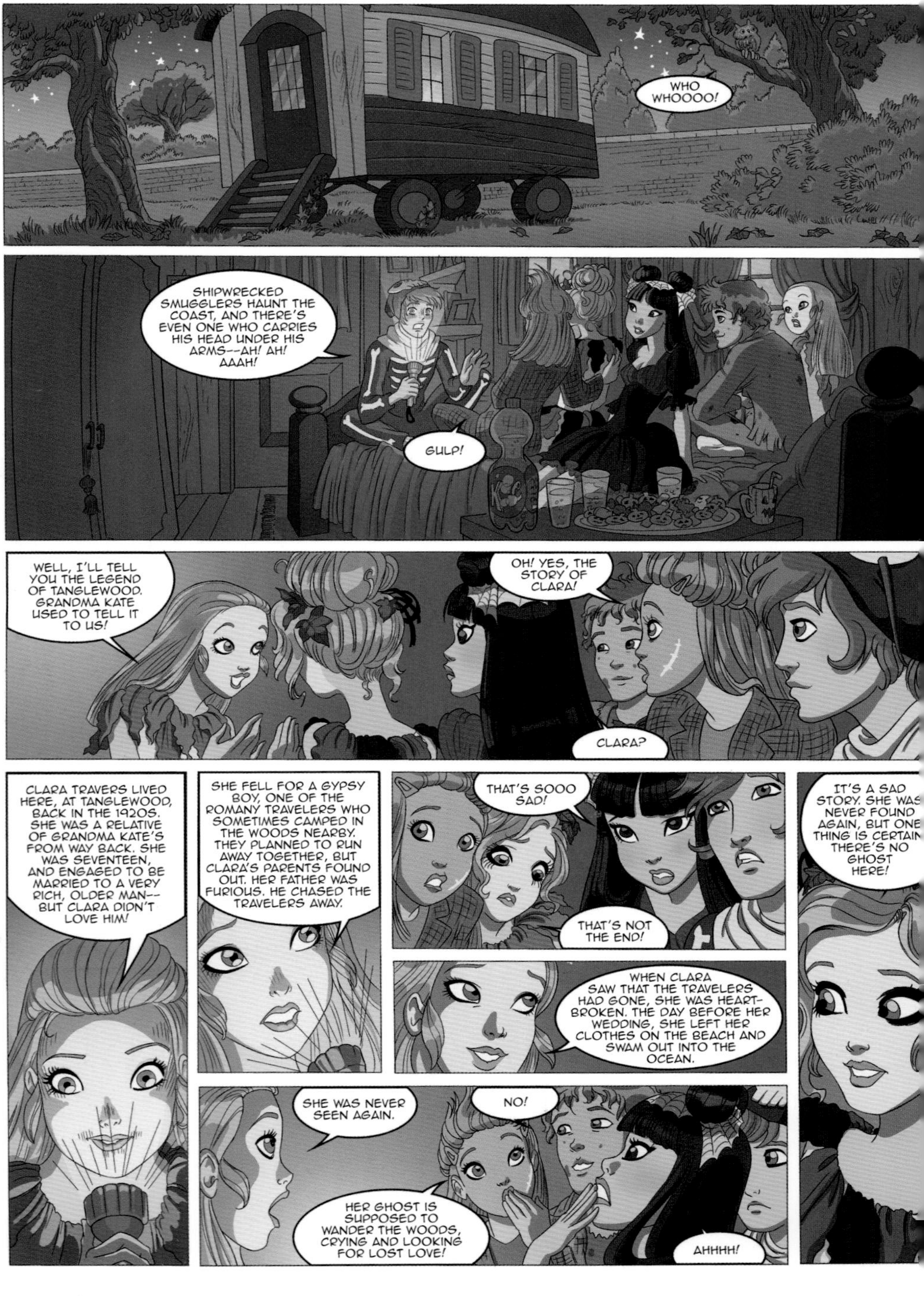
WHO WHOOOO!
SHIPWRECKED SMUGGLERS HAUNT THE COAST, AND THERE'S EVEN ONE WHO CARRIES HIS HEAD UNDER HIS ARMS--AH! AH! AAAH!
GULP!
WELL, I'LL TELL YOU THE LEGEND OF TANGLEWOOD. GRANDMA KATE USED TO TELL IT TO US!
OH! YES, THE STORY OF CLARA!
CLARA?
CLARA TRAVERS LIVED HERE, AT TANGLEWOOD, BACK IN THE 1920S. SHE WAS A RELATIVE OF GRANDMA KATE'S FROM WAY BACK. SHE WAS SEVENTEEN, AND ENGAGED TO BE MARRIED TO A VERY RICH, OLDER MAN--BUT CLARA DIDN'T LOVE HIM!
SHE FELL FOR A GYPSY BOY, ONE OF THE ROMANY TRAVELERS WHO SOMETIMES CAMPED IN THE WOODS NEARBY. THEY PLANNED TO RUN AWAY TOGETHER, BUT CLARA'S PARENTS FOUND OUT. HER FATHER WAS FURIOUS. HE CHASED THE TRAVELERS AWAY.
THAT'S SOOO SAD!
THAT'S NOT THE END!
WHEN CLARA SAW THAT THE TRAVELERS HAD GONE, SHE WAS HEART-BROKEN. THE DAY BEFORE HER WEDDING, SHE LEFT HER CLOTHES ON THE BEACH AND SWAM OUT INTO THE OCEAN.
SHE WAS NEVER SEEN AGAIN.
NO!
HER GHOST IS SUPPOSED TO WANDER THE WOODS, CRYING AND LOOKING FOR LOST LOVE!
AHHHH!
IT'S A SAD STORY. SHE WAS NEVER FOUND AGAIN, BUT ONE THING IS CERTAIN THERE'S NO GHOST HERE!

THE NEXT MORNING.

WHAT'S ALL THIS?

DAD AND CHARLOTTE HAVE BEGUN TO CLEAR THE ATTIC FOR MY BEDROOM. IT'LL BE COLD IN THE WINTER IN THE CARAVAN!

I DON'T SUPPOSE YOU REMEMBER THAT OLD STORY YOUR GRAN USED TO TELL?

A SAD STORY ABOUT CLARA TRAVERS? I THINK THESE LETTERS BELONGED TO HER!

MOM, CAN I HAVE THAT BIRDCAGE?

AND ME, THE VIOLIN, PLEASE!

OK, THEN! SO LONG AS CHERRY AND SKYE PICK SOMETHING, TOO!

MOM, DO YOU THINK THESE CLOTHES BELONGED TO CLARA TRAVERS?

YES!

THANKS, CHARLOTTE, BUT I DON'T LIKE OLD THINGS!

SUMMER, WILL YOU HELP ME CARRY CLARA'S TRUNK INTO THE BEDROOM?

YES, IF YOU WANT.

SKYE, YOU LOVE VINTAGE CLOTHES, DON'T YOU? I THINK CLARA WOULD HAVE WANTED YOU TO HAVE THEM! AND HONEY WON'T WANT THEM, SHE'S STILL POUTING IN HER BEDROOM!

WHO WANTS TO TASTE MY MARSH-MALLOW?

AH! NO-- MARSHMALLOW'S ANYTHING BUT BLAND! IT'S SWEET, LIGHT, LIKE A LITTLE BIT OF PARADISE!

I DON'T LIKE IT! IT'S BLAND!

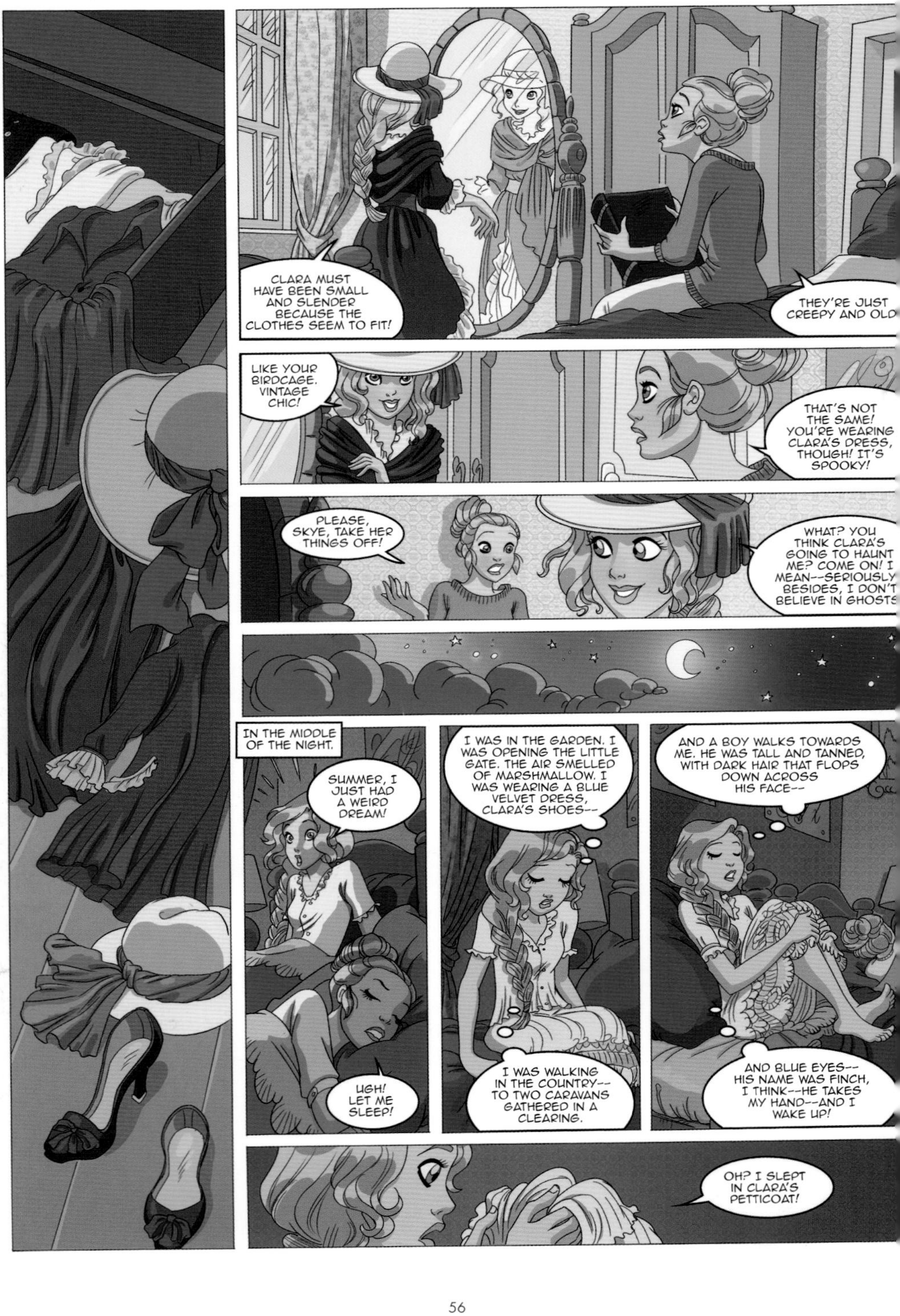
CLARA MUST HAVE BEEN SMALL AND SLENDER BECAUSE THE CLOTHES SEEM TO FIT!
THEY'RE JUST CREEPY AND OLD
LIKE YOUR BIRDCAGE. VINTAGE CHIC!
THAT'S NOT THE SAME! YOU'RE WEARING CLARA'S DRESS, THOUGH! IT'S SPOOKY!
PLEASE, SKYE, TAKE HER THINGS OFF!
WHAT? YOU THINK CLARA'S GOING TO HAUNT ME? COME ON! I MEAN--SERIOUSLY. BESIDES, I DON'T BELIEVE IN GHOSTS
IN THE MIDDLE OF THE NIGHT.
SUMMER, I JUST HAD A WEIRD DREAM!
UGH! LET ME SLEEP!
I WAS IN THE GARDEN. I WAS OPENING THE LITTLE GATE. THE AIR SMELLED OF MARSHMALLOW. I WAS WEARING A BLUE VELVET DRESS, CLARA'S SHOES--
I WAS WALKING IN THE COUNTRY--TO TWO CARAVANS GATHERED IN A CLEARING.
AND A BOY WALKS TOWARDS ME. HE WAS TALL AND TANNED, WITH DARK HAIR THAT FLOPS DOWN ACROSS HIS FACE--
AND BLUE EYES--HIS NAME WAS FINCH, I THINK--HE TAKES MY HAND--AND I WAKE UP!
OH? I SLEPT IN CLARA'S PETTICOAT!

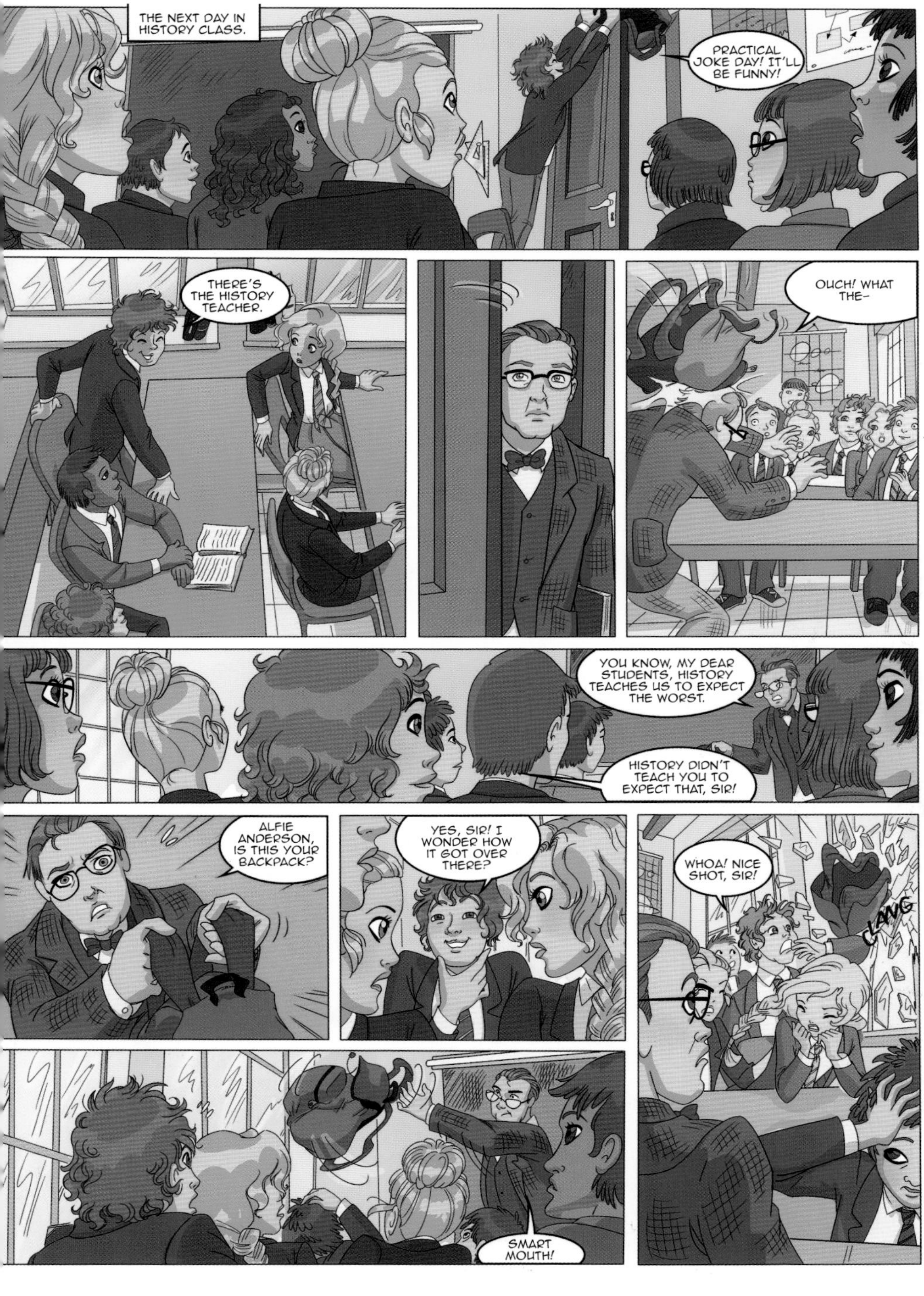
THE NEXT DAY IN HISTORY CLASS.
PRACTICAL JOKE DAY! IT'LL BE FUNNY!
THERE'S THE HISTORY TEACHER.
OUCH! WHAT THE-
YOU KNOW, MY DEAR STUDENTS, HISTORY TEACHES US TO EXPECT THE WORST.
HISTORY DIDN'T TEACH YOU TO EXPECT THAT, SIR!
ALFIE ANDERSON, IS THIS YOUR BACKPACK?
YES, SIR! I WONDER HOW IT GOT OVER THERE?
SMART MOUTH!
WHOA! NICE SHOT, SIR!
CLANG

OWW!

ALFIE, SEE WHAT YOU'VE DONE WITH YOUR ROTTEN JOKES?

YEAH, WAY TO GO, ALFIE!

I DIDN'T BREAK THE WINDOW!

THIS JUST HIT ME IN THE HEAD!

WHO DID THIS?

IT WAS ME, SIR. I WAS MESSING AROUND AND MR. WOLFE TOLD ME TO STOP AND--IT WAS AN ACCIDENT, SIR, BUT IT IS MY FAULT.

MY OFFICE, NOW, ALFIE!

HISTORY ISN'T ALWAYS WHAT IT SEEMS, AND IT'S ALL TOO EASY TO GET THE WRONG IDEA.

YOU HAVE TO PIECE TOGETHER THE CLUES TO MAKE SENSE OF IT ALL.

I'D BETTER SET THE RECORD STRAIGHT. I CAN'T LET ALFIE TAKE THE BLAME FOR THIS!

WHAT HE JUST SAID MAKES ME THINK ABOUT CLARA TRAVERS. I SHOULD SEARCH FOR CLUES TO PIECE TOGETHER HER STORY. MY DREAM WAS SO VIVID! WHAT IF I'M HAUNTED BY CLARA?

LATER, IN THE CAFETERIA.

THE HISTORY TEACHER WAS COOL! HE TOLD THE PRINCIPAL EVERYTHING. I COULD HAVE BEEN KICKED OUT. I JUST HAVE DETENTION FOR ONE HOUR AFTER CLASSES FOR A WEEK.

I THOUGHT YOU WERE A VEGETARIAN, SINCE YOUR PARENTS RUN THE HEALTH-FOOD STORE!

YOU GOT THE STEAK AND FRIES?

I DON'T EAT ONLY SALAD BECAUSE MY PARENTS ARE OLD HIPPIES WHO SMELL OF PATCHOULI AND WEAR HAND-KNITTED SWEATERS!

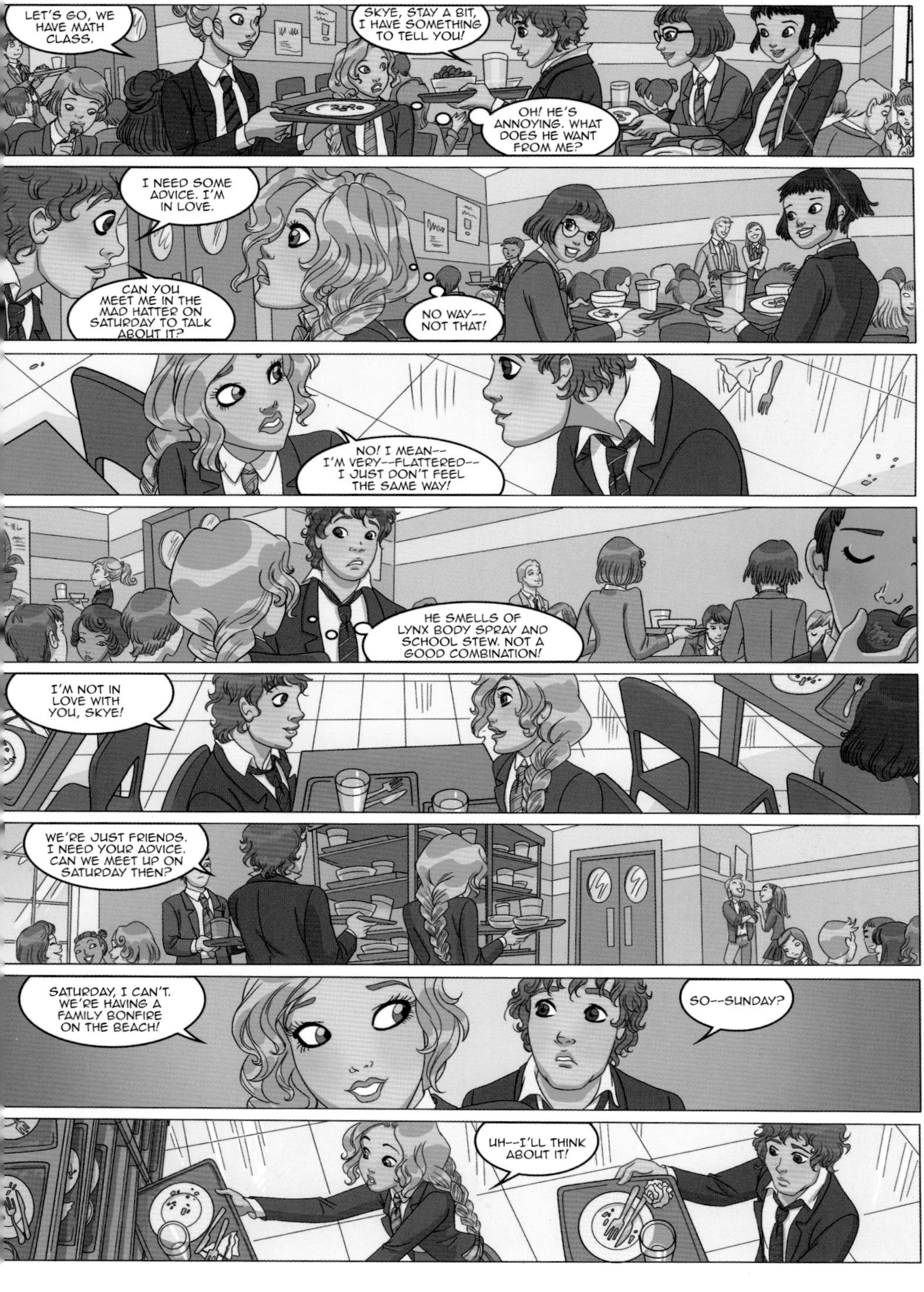
LET'S GO, WE HAVE MATH CLASS.
SKYE, STAY A BIT, I HAVE SOMETHING TO TELL YOU!
OH! HE'S ANNOYING. WHAT DOES HE WANT FROM ME?
I NEED SOME ADVICE. I'M IN LOVE.
CAN YOU MEET ME IN THE MAD HATTER ON SATURDAY TO TALK ABOUT IT?
NO WAY-- NOT THAT!
NO! I MEAN-- I'M VERY--FLATTERED-- I JUST DON'T FEEL THE SAME WAY!
HE SMELLS OF LYNX BODY SPRAY AND SCHOOL STEW. NOT A GOOD COMBINATION!
I'M NOT IN LOVE WITH YOU, SKYE!
WE'RE JUST FRIENDS. I NEED YOUR ADVICE. CAN WE MEET UP ON SATURDAY THEN?
SATURDAY, I CAN'T. WE'RE HAVING A FAMILY BONFIRE ON THE BEACH!
SO--SUNDAY?
UH--I'LL THINK ABOUT IT!

SATURDAY NIGHT.

THERE'S A RUMOR AT SCHOOL THAT ALFIE HAS A CRUSH ON YOU!

WHATEVER, HE FANCIES SOMEONE ELSE!

HE WANTS TO SEE ME TO ASK FOR ADVICE. HE'S IN LOVE!

YEAH, RIGHT!

I'M HAPPY YOU'RE HERE, HONEY!

MOM MADE SUCH A FUSS. THIS BIG LECTURE ABOUT BEING A PART OF THE FAMILY AND GIVING PADDY AND CHERRY A CHANCE.

CHERRY PLAYS IT COOL. SHE PLAYS HER CARDS CLOSE. SHE STOLE SHAY FROM ME, YOU MUSTN'T FORGET! SHE'LL NEVER BE MY SISTER, AND PADDY WILL NEVER REPLACE DAD!

I KNOW SHE'S HURT YOU, BUT SHE DIDN'T PLAN ANY OF THAT. REMEMBER, YOU WEREN'T GOING WITH SHAY ANY LONGER. YOU WERE SO MEAN TO HIM!

BOY, HAS SHE GOT YOU SUCKERED!

IF YOU ACTUALLY GOT TO KNOW HER––

WHAT DID YOU SAY TO HONEY, SKYE? SHE WAS CRYING! WHY DID YOU HAVE TO UPSET HER?

I JUST SAID SHE SHOULD GIVE CHERRY A CHANCE!

IT WAS COOL LAST NIGHT WHEN WE DANCED AROUND THE FIRE!

WHAT ARE YOU TALKING ABOUT?

WE DIDN'T DANCE AROUND THE FIRE LAST NIGHT?

NOPE!

BUT IT SEEMED SO REAL--I DANCED AROUND A FIRE WITH THAT BOY--FINCH?

I--I THINK I DREAMT ABOUT CLARA AND THE GYPSIES. WELL, I WAS IN CLARA'S PLACE!

NOW DO YOU UNDERSTAND WHY I WANT YOU TO GET RID OF THOSE OLD CLOTHES? YOU THINK YOU'RE THAT GIRL-- FORGET ALL THAT, OK?

I DON'T WANT TO LET GO OF CLARA'S STORY.

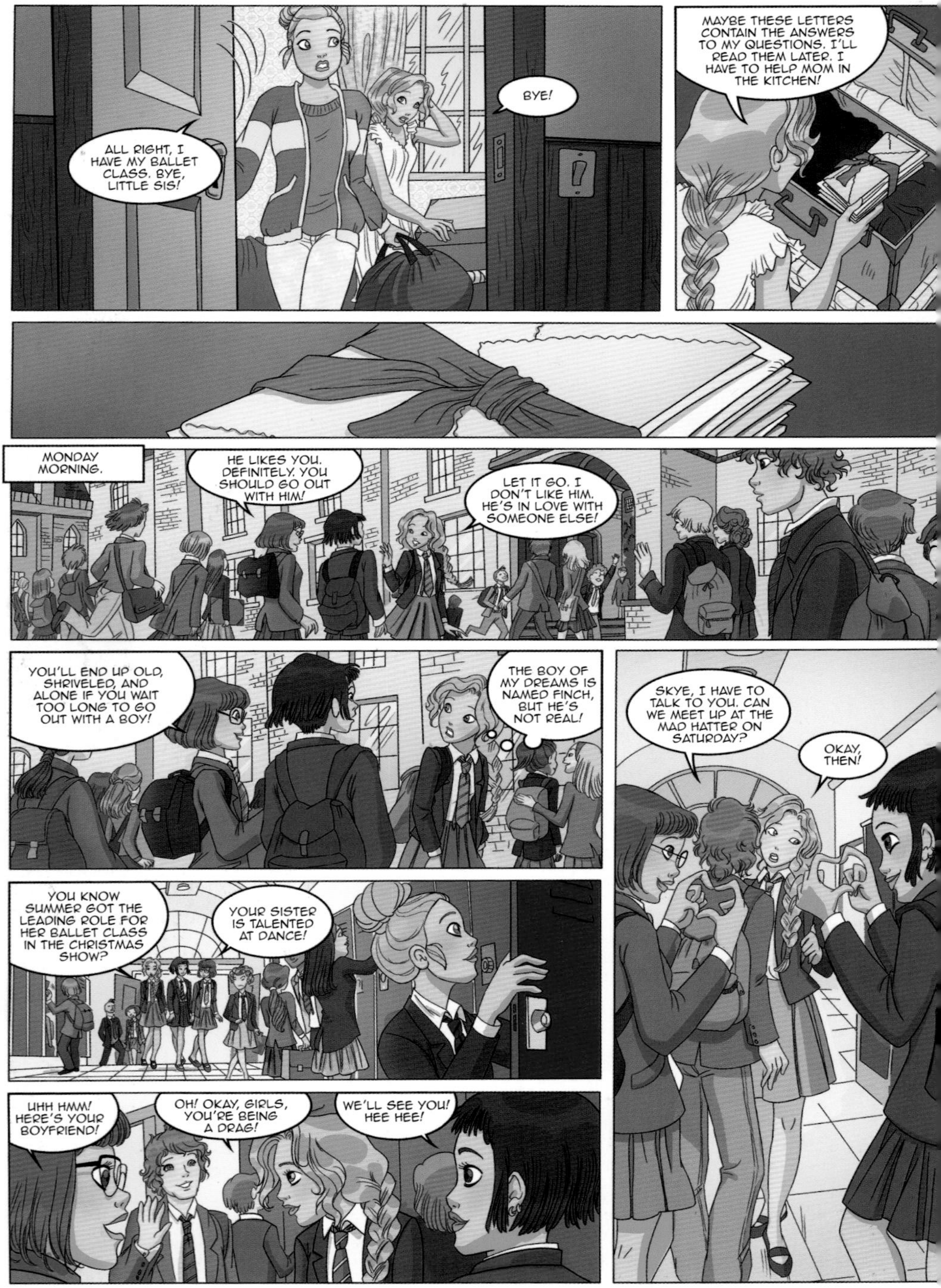

ALL RIGHT, I HAVE MY BALLET CLASS. BYE, LITTLE SIS!
BYE!
MAYBE THESE LETTERS CONTAIN THE ANSWERS TO MY QUESTIONS. I'LL READ THEM LATER. I HAVE TO HELP MOM IN THE KITCHEN!
MONDAY MORNING.
HE LIKES YOU. DEFINITELY. YOU SHOULD GO OUT WITH HIM!
LET IT GO. I DON'T LIKE HIM. HE'S IN LOVE WITH SOMEONE ELSE!
YOU'LL END UP OLD, SHRIVELED, AND ALONE IF YOU WAIT TOO LONG TO GO OUT WITH A BOY!
THE BOY OF MY DREAMS IS NAMED FINCH, BUT HE'S NOT REAL!
YOU KNOW SUMMER GOT THE LEADING ROLE FOR HER BALLET CLASS IN THE CHRISTMAS SHOW?
YOUR SISTER IS TALENTED AT DANCE!
UHH HMM! HERE'S YOUR BOYFRIEND!
OH! OKAY, GIRLS, YOU'RE BEING A DRAG!
WE'LL SEE YOU! HEE HEE!
SKYE, I HAVE TO TALK TO YOU. CAN WE MEET UP AT THE MAD HATTER ON SATURDAY?
OKAY, THEN!

SATURDAY AFTERNOON.

OK, SKYE, I NEED YOUR HELP!

YOU'RE A GIRL, SO YOU MIGHT BE ABLE TO TELL ME WHERE I'M GOING WRONG. I HAVE A PLAN, AND YOU CAN HELP ME MAKE IT HAPPEN. THE THING IS--I WANT TO BE IRRESISTIBLE TO WOMEN!

PFFFFFFF!

WHAT? IS THAT FUNNY OR SOMETHING?

NO, NO, I WASN'T LAUGHING. IT'S JUST SOMETHING WENT DOWN THE WRONG WAY.

YEAH, RIGHT. THAT'S EXACTLY THE PROBLEM. I'VE LIKED THIS GIRL FOR A WHILE, BUT SHE THINKS I'M AN IDIOT. I'M TIRED OF IT!

GIRLS ARE A BIT OF A MYSTERY TO ME. I'D LIKE TO LEARN A LITTLE MORE ABOUT WHAT MAKES THEM HAPPY.

OK, I'LL GIVE YOU SOME FRIENDLY ADVICE!

OK, FIRST, WHAT'S OFF WITH ME?

YOU'RE TAKING NOTES? SERIOUSLY?

OK, THEN--HAIR. DITCH THE GEL. YOU LOOK LIKE A MANIAC!

BUT--I GOT THIS LOOK OUT OF A FASHION MAG!

IT'S A FLOP. YOU LOOK LIKE YOU IRONED YOUR FRINGE IN SEVEN DIFFERENT DIRECTIONS, THEN HAD A FIGHT WITH A TUBE OF GEL. TRUST ME, IT'S NOT A GOOD LOOK.

OK. ANYTHING ELSE?

NO MORE CLOWNING AROUND IN CLASS. THAT'S IMPORTANT. IT'S KIND OF CHILDISH. YOU'RE THIRTEEN NOW. PRACTICAL JOKES AREN'T FUNNY ANYMORE!

BUT I THOUGHT GIRLS LIKED FUNNY BOYS?

NOK NOK

COCO, GET LOST!

YOUR SISTER'S GIVING YOU A HARD TIME?

SUMMER, TOO?

SUMMER? SHE THINKS IT'S HUGELY FUNNY YOU'RE HANGING AROUND ME. SHE THINKS YOU FANCY ME.

MAYBE SHE'S JUST A BIT JEALOUS?

ALFIE'S MYSTERY GIRL IS SUMMER!

YOU'RE FAMOUS, GIRLS!

YEAH! IT'S THE FEATURE ON THIS SUMMER'S CHOCOLATE FESTIVAL!

OH! HERE'S THE PHOTO OF US DRESSED AS CHOCOLATE FAIRIES!

THE CHOCOLATE BOX

WE LOOK GREAT! LIKE PROPER SISTERS!

WE ARE PROPER SISTERS. DEFINITELY!

THE WRITE-UP TALKS ABOUT THE TRUFFLES BEING HANDMADE, AND THE BOXES HAND-PAINTED.

BEST OF ALL, IT SAYS THEY TASTE AMAZING!

IT'S GREAT PUBLICITY!

I'M RELIEVED. I KNOW THAT MOM AND PADDY HAVE BEEN STRUGGLING WITH MONEY--

THE B&B DOESN'T DO WELL IN THE WINTER!

GET GOING, THEN! GIRLS, YOU HAVE SCHOOL. YOU'LL BE LATE. AND I HAVE BREAKFAST TO FIX FOR THE GUESTS WHO ARRIVED YESTERDAY!

YEAH, OUR ONLY TWO CUSTOMERS AT THE MOMENT!

AT THE HIGH SCHOOL.

IT'S OFFICIAL. HONEY HAS DUMPED HER BOYFRIEND ALEX.

OH! I DIDN'T KNOW! WE HARDLY EVER SEE HER AT HOME.

SHE HAS SUCH A HECTIC SOCIAL LIFE IT'S STARTING TO FEEL LIKE SHE IS ONE OF THE B&B GUESTS!

HEY, CHOCOLATE BOX GIRLS! GREAT ARTICLE ABOUT YOU!

THANKS, MILLIE! YEAH, IT'S COOL!

MY MOM JUST ORDERED FIVE BOXES OF CHOCOLATE FOR CHRISTMAS!

OH! THANKS! PADDY WILL GET IT DONE!

WALKING IN FRONT OF THE STAFFROOM, I HEARD MR. WOLFE ORDERED A BOX FOR HIS FIANCÉE!

MR. WOLFE HAS A FIANCÉE?

WELL, YEAH-- YOU SEE, SKYE, EVERYBODY HAS SOMEONE! EXCEPT YOU!

I DO HAVE SOMEONE--IN MY DREAMS!

HEY HO! SKYE-- WAKE UP! YOU DIDN'T HEAR THE ALARM?

HUH? WHAT?

KEEPING MY DREAMS ALL TO MYSELF, IT'S SO HARD COMING BACK TO REALITY!

SUMMER, YOU KNOW THOSE OLD LETTERS FROM THE TRUNK? HAVE YOU SEEN THEM AT ALL?

WHAT LETTERS?

YOU KNOW-- THE BUNDLE OF CLARA TRAVERS' LETTERS. I CAN'T FIND THEM!

LOOK, I DON'T KNOW WHERE THEY ARE! I DIDN'T TOUCH THEM! WHY WOULD I BE INTERESTED IN SPOOKY, OLD LETTERS?

I'M NOT BLAMING YOU, SUMMER, I'M JUST BUGGING ME THAT I'VE LOST THEM!

LATER, IN THE KITCHEN.

AFTER SCHOOL, GIRLS, COME GIVE US A HAND TO FILL THE CHOCOLATE BOXES. THANKS TO THE ARTICLE, ORDERS ARE NON-STOP!

CERTAINLY NOT! THAT'S SLAVERY!

HONEY, YOU'RE GETTING MORE AND MORE UNPLEASANT!

WHAT MOM SAYS IS TRUE. YOU NEVER USED TO BE LIKE THIS. I USED TO LOOK UP TO YOU. I THOUGHT YOU WERE THE COOLEST BIG SISTER IN THE WORLD--

BUT I WAS WRONG. YOU'RE NOT COOL AT ALL--YOU'RE SHALLOW AND SPITEFUL AND CRUEL!

WHAT DID YOU HAVE TO GO AND SAY THAT FOR?

IT'S JUST-- SHE NEVER HELPS. SHE'S NEVER HERE.

MAYBE YOU ACTUALLY GOT THROUGH TO HER? I'M NOT GETTING THINGS RIGHT WITH HONEY. PERHAPS WE NEED TO TAKE A HARDER LINE--FOR HER OWN SAKE.

MORE CHOCOLATE ORDERS? WOW!

WHO CAN GO BY THE POST OFFICE AFTER SCHOOL? TO SEND THESE THREE BOXES?

I CAN'T. I HAVE DANCE CLASS.

I'LL DO IT!

LATER THAT AFTERNOON.

AFTER WHAT I SAID TO HONEY THIS MORNING, I THINK SUMMER'S MAD AT ME!

POST OFFICE

SKYE, I'M SENSING A SADNESS ABOUT YOU TODAY!

HELLO, MRS. LEE. YES, I'M NOT IN A GREAT MOOD.

YOU KNOW, I HAVE A GIFT. MY MOTHER WAS HALF-GYPSY AND SHE GAVE ME THE GIFT OF READING PALMS. GIVE ME YOUR HAND!

I SEE ROMANCE! A BOY!

I'M NOT ALL THAT INTERESTED IN BOYS, REALLY!

I SEE--HE'S WEARING A RED SCARF!

DID SHE SEE FINCH?

IF MRS. LEE IS RIGHT--HOW CAN A BOY WHO BELONGS IN THE PAST BE A PART OF MY FUTURE?

HI, SKYE!

SKYE! HOW'S IT GOING? WANT TO COME TO THE PARK WITH ME?

HI, ALFIE. IT'S COLD AND IT'LL BE GETTING DARK SOON!

CHRISTMAS IS IN A MONTH. WHAT DO YOU WANT FOR A GIFT?

WHAT YOU'RE REALLY INTERESTED IN IS WHAT SUMMER WANTS FOR CHRISTMAS, EH?

I WONDER HOW HE'D FEEL IF HE KNEW SUMMER THINKS HE'S LIKE A SMALL, ANNOYING, INSECT, BUZZING AROUND YOUR EARS.

SHE WON'T BE EXPECTING A GIFT FROM YOU!

I WAS GOING TO LEAVE IT IN HER LOCKER AT SCHOOL, WITHOUT SIGNING IT, AND SHE'D KNOW SHE HAD A SECRET ADMIRER!

DO YOU THINK SHE'D LIKE THIS?

UH--IT'S PERFECT! AND DON'T WORRY, I WON'T SAY ANYTHING!

I HAVE TO SAY GOOD-BYE. I'M GOING TO BUY A CHOCOLATE ÉCLAIR FOR HONEY. I WAS A BIT HARD ON HER THIS MORNING!

YOU'RE REALLY A GOOD FRIEND! DID YOU SEE? I FOLLOWED YOUR ADVICE ABOUT MY HAIR. I'M NOT USING GEL ANY LONGER.

YEAH, I SAW!!

LATER, AT DINNER TIME.

SUMMER, I FEEL BAD. I REGRET SAYING THOSE THINGS TO HONEY THIS MORNING AND--I HATE IT WHEN WE QUARREL!

I'M SORRY FOR SNAPPING AT YOU. IT WAS JUST A SURPRISE BECAUSE USUALLY YOU'RE TRYING TO KEEP THE PEACE! YOU'RE SO DIFFERENT NOW!

LATELY--WELL, YOU'RE CHALLENGING HONEY. SAYING WHAT YOU THINK.

CLARA WASN'T THE KIND TO BE QUIET EITHER!

SUMMER HAS ALWAYS STRUGGLED WITH THE IDEA THAT IDENTICAL TWINS MIGHT NOT ALWAYS HAVE IDENTICAL FEELINGS AND VIEWS!

SKYE--I WAS WONDERING--IS EVERYTHING OK WITH YOU AND MILLIE?

WHY DO YOU ASK?

WELL, YOU KNOW I'M CLOSE TO TINA, AND YOU'RE CLOSE TO MILLIE. AND LATELY, MILLIE IS ALWAYS HANGING AROUND TINA AND ME!

YOU KNOW, MILLIE HAS ALWAYS LIKED YOU IN A STAR-STRUCK WAY!

WHATEVER!

I'M STARTING TO FEEL MORE AND MORE LIKE A SHADOW GIRL.

EVERYBODY IS CRAZY ABOUT HER--FIRST ALFIE, AND NOW MILLIE!

A FEW DAYS BEFORE CHRISTMAS.

I'D QUITE LIKE A CHRISTMAS EVE PARTY WITH OUR FRIENDS AND NEIGHBORS!

AND NUT ROAST INSTEAD OF TURKEY BECAUSE I'M A VEGETARIAN NOW!

THE NEXT DAY AT SCHOOL.

WHAT'S THIS GIFT?

THE LOCKERS DON'T LOCK, SO ANYBODY CAN OPEN THEM!

AND YOU'LL COME AND SEE ME IN THE DANCE-SCHOOL CHRISTMAS SPECIAL? IT'LL BE AWESOME!

WOW! IT'S BEAUTIFUL!

YOU FORGOT THE CARD THAT GOES WITH IT!

A secret admirer

I HAVE NO IDEA WHO IT COULD BE!

THIS IS SO, SO ROMANTIC!

COULD IT BE AARON JONES?

OR SOMEONE ELSE?

SKYE, IT MAKES ME FEEL ALL TINGLY AND HAPPY INSIDE TO KNOW THAT SOMEBODY--WELL, Y'KNOW--LIKES ME!

I THOUGHT YOU WEREN'T INTERESTED IN BOYS, JUST BALLET!

I'M NOT. JUST-- CURIOUS, Y'KNOW! YOU WOULD BE, TOO, IF IT WAS YOU!

IT'S NOT ME, THOUGH, IS IT?

IT WILL BE. SOON, I BET. A BOY WILL GIVE YOU A GIFT, TOO!

YES. SUMMER'S RIGHT. WE GROW UP AT OUR OWN PACE, ALL THE MAGAZINES SAY SO. I EXPECT YOU'LL CATCH UP SOON, SKYE!

MILLIE'S ANNOYING ME MORE AND MORE. GROWING UP ISN'T ALL ABOUT GLITTERY LIP GLOSS AND CLUMPY SHOES AND GIGGLING WHENEVER A BOY LOOKS IN YOUR DIRECTION!

I HAVE A SECRET CRUSH ON SOMEONE WHO'S UNATTAINABLE. I DON'T BELIEVE IN GHOSTS, SO HOW COME I'M CRUSHING ON ONE?

LET'S MEET AT LUNCHTIME. WE CAN MAKE A LIST OF POSSIBLE BOYS.

MAYBE IT'S ALFIE ANDERSON!

RIGHT! IF HE WAS TRYING TO IMPRESS SOMEONE, HE'D GIVE THEM CHEWING GUM THAT MADE THEIR TONGUE GO BLUE OR A STINK BOMB!

HEE HEE HEE!

THIS IS ANNOYING. MILLIE'S DRIFTING AWAY FROM ME, AND I FEEL SORRY FOR POOR ALFIE. IF HE KNEW WHAT SUMMER THOUGHT OF HIM!

HEE HEE HEE!

WOW! YOUR NEW BEDROOM IN THE ATTIC IS SO COOL!

CHARLOTTE AND PADDY WERE AWESOME-- IT STILL SMELLS A LITTLE OF PAINT!

SKYE? ARE YOU LOST IN THOUGHT? ARE YOU OKAY?

AM I THE ONE FINCH KISSED THAT NIGHT IN MY DREAM OR CLARA TRAVERS? I DON'T KNOW ANYMORE!

SKYE!!! IT'S LIKE YOU'RE OFF IN YOUR OWN WORLD LATELY!

UH--MY FRIEND MILLIE'S ALWAYS WITH SUMMER, AND SUMMER ONLY THINKS ABOUT DANCE--SO--UH--UH--

DO YOU BELIEVE IN GHOSTS?

GHOSTS?

WELL, YOU KNOW. SPIRITS FROM THE PAST.

YOU KNOW, CHERRY, LATELY, I'VE BEEN HAVING THESE STRANGE DREAMS, LIKE SNAPSHOTS OF THE PAST-- ABOUT THE GYPSIES IN THE WOODS. IT HAS TO BE LINKED WITH CLARA TRAVERS. YOU KNOW, THE GIRL WHO DISAPPEARED.

THEY'RE DREAMS, THOUGH. THAT'S NOT THE SAME AS ACTUALLY SEEING GHOSTS, IS IT?

YES, BUT IT'S LIKE IN THOSE SPOOKY MOVIES SOME GHOST IS LINGERING ON BECAUSE THEY WANT PEOPLE TO DISCOVER THE TRUTH ABOUT WHAT REALLY HAPPENED IN THE PAST. IT FEELS A BIT LIKE THAT!

YOU THINK CLARA'S TRYING TO TELL YOU SOMETHING?

LIKE--MAYBE SHE DIDN'T KILL HERSELF AFTER ALL? MAYBE SHE WAS--MURDERED? SCARY!

NO, IT'S NOT SCARY AT ALL. BUT THERE MUST BE SOMETHING, SURELY? SOME REASON I CAN'T LET GO OF IT?

CLARA'S STORY HAS REALLY HIT HOME FOR YOU.

DID YOU KNOW RIGHT FROM THE START THAT YOU LIKED SHAY?

NO WAY! I THOUGHT HE WAS VAIN AND ARROGANT AND ANNOYING AND ALSO, HE WAS HONEY'S BOYFRIEND!

THEN HE BROKE UP WITH YOUR SISTER AND I GOT TO KNOW HIM. HAD FEELINGS FOR HIM. AND HIM, TOO. WHY DO YOU ASK? IS THERE SOMEONE YOU LIKE, TOO--ALFIE?

NO, NO, NOT ALFIE. DEFINITELY NOT ALFIE--IT'S COMPLICATED.

IT'S ALWAYS COMPLICATED!

LATER, IN SUMMER AND SKYE'S BEDROOM.

SKYE! I HAVE A BRILLIANT IDEA! FOR CHRISTMAS, WE COULD ASK FOR A BIRTHDAY PARTY. A SPECIAL ONE FOR OUR THIRTEENTH. WHAT DO YOU THINK?

WHAT DO I THINK? CAKE AND HOT CHOCOLATE IN THE MAD HATTER WOULD SUIT ME WAY BETTER THAN SOME AWKWARD TEEN PARTY WHERE GIRLS DRESS UP, SIP COKE, AND EYE BOYS!

I THINK IT SOUNDS LIKE TORTURE, BUT SUMMER CLEARLY DOESN'T!

CHRISTMAS EVE.

I LOVE GOING TO THE THEATER!

MAYBE ONE DAY SUMMER WILL BECOME A PRIMA BALLERINA!

HONEY COULD'VE COME, ALL THE SAME!

SHE'S AMAZING!

I KNOW!

I INVITED ALFIE AND HIS PARENTS TO THE CHRISTMAS PARTY TOMORROW EVENING.

WHAT?

MAYBE I WOULD HAVE STUCK WITH BALLET IF I HADN'T FELT LIKE I WAS IN SUMMER'S SHADOW!

SUMMER IS REALLY TALENTED AT DANCE. SHE'S AMAZING!

BRAVO!

THE EVENING OF THE TANGLEWOOD CHRISTMAS PARTY.

I LIKE THAT FLOWER THING IN YOUR HAIR. WHERE DID YOU GET IT?

FROM A CLOSE FRIEND! COULD YOU MOVE ASIDE A LITTLE? YOU'RE IN MY WAY!

DID YOU HEAR THAT? SUMMER SEES ME AS A CLOSE FRIEND!

DON'T GET YOUR HOPES UP!

SHE MADE A LIST OF POSSIBLE ADMIRERS, AND YOU WEREN'T EVEN ON IT!

LATER THAT EVENING.

ALFIE? WHAT ARE YOU DOING HERE?

KEEPING A LOOKOUT FOR FLYING REINDEER. YOU?

THE PARTY'S WINDING DOWN. I WANTED SOME FRESH AIR!

I'M INVISIBLE. I TRIED TO KISS SUMMER UNDER THE MISTLETOE AND SHE TOLD ME TO GET LOST!

WHAT ABOUT YOU, SKYE? MIGHT BE A WAY TO KEEP WARM!

THAT'S NOT FUNNY! EVEN IF WE'RE IDENTICAL TWINS, I'M NOT SUMMER!

YOU CAN'T KISS ME INSTEAD OF HER BECAUSE WE LOOK ALIKE!

YOU FANCY SUMMER, NOT ME!

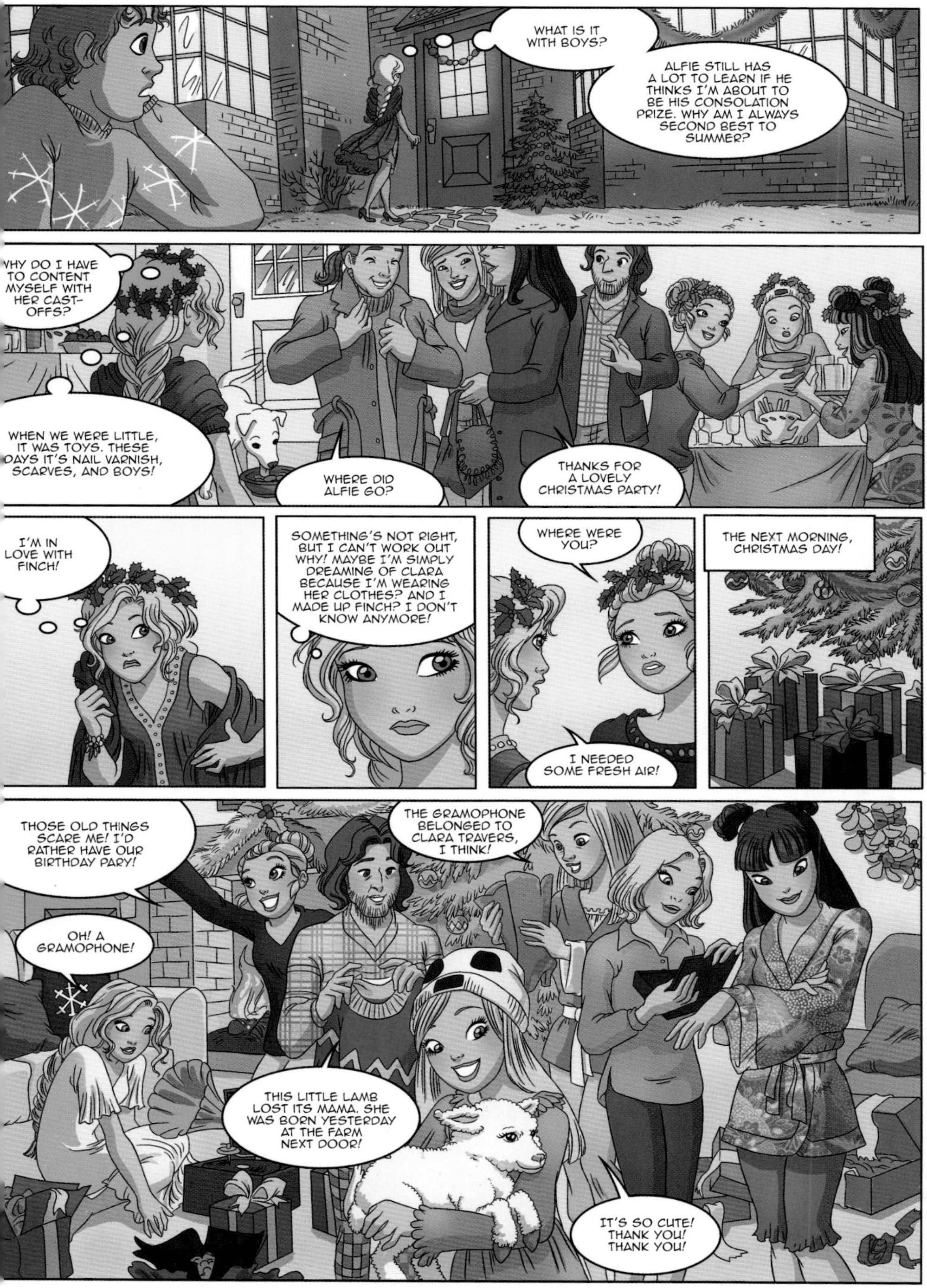
WHAT IS IT WITH BOYS?
ALFIE STILL HAS A LOT TO LEARN IF HE THINKS I'M ABOUT TO BE HIS CONSOLATION PRIZE. WHY AM I ALWAYS SECOND BEST TO SUMMER?
WHY DO I HAVE TO CONTENT MYSELF WITH HER CAST-OFFS?
WHEN WE WERE LITTLE, IT WAS TOYS. THESE DAYS IT'S NAIL VARNISH, SCARVES, AND BOYS!
WHERE DID ALFIE GO?
THANKS FOR A LOVELY CHRISTMAS PARTY!
I'M IN LOVE WITH FINCH!
SOMETHING'S NOT RIGHT, BUT I CAN'T WORK OUT WHY! MAYBE I'M SIMPLY DREAMING OF CLARA BECAUSE I'M WEARING HER CLOTHES? AND I MADE UP FINCH? I DON'T KNOW ANYMORE!
WHERE WERE YOU?
I NEEDED SOME FRESH AIR!
THE NEXT MORNING, CHRISTMAS DAY!
THOSE OLD THINGS SCARE ME! I'D RATHER HAVE OUR BIRTHDAY PARY!
THE GRAMOPHONE BELONGED TO CLARA TRAVERS, I THINK!
OH! A GRAMOPHONE!
THIS LITTLE LAMB LOST ITS MAMA. SHE WAS BORN YESTERDAY AT THE FARM NEXT DOOR!
IT'S SO CUTE! THANK YOU! THANK YOU!

COCO, PADDY CLEANED OUT THE OLD SHED IN THE YARD. THAT'LL MAKE A LITTLE HOUSE FOR YOUR LAMB!

I'LL CALL IT "MERRY CHRISTMAS"!

DAD'S ON SKYPE TO WISH US A HAPPY CHRISTMAS!

MERRY CHRISTMAS, DAD!

YOU'RE LOOKING SO GROWN UP!

WHAT TIME IS IT IN AUSTRALIA?

IT'S EVENING NOW--THE WEATHER IS FANTASTIC! YOU'LL HAVE TO COME OUT AND VISIT!

I'D LOVE TO SEE AUSTRALIA, IT HAS TO BE BETTER THAN THIS DUMP. WHEN WOULD BE A GOOD TIME?

BETTER WAIT UNTIL WE'VE SETTLED IN A BIT! GIVE YOUR MOM A CHANCE TO SAVE UP THE AIRFARES! GIRLS, IT'S BEEN GREAT TALKING TO YOU! BYE!

HE HAS A GIRLFRIEND, I'M SURE OF IT! HE SAID "WE."

NO WAY, HE WOULDN'T!

IF MOM HAS TO PAY FOR THE PLANE TICKETS, WE WON'T GO SEE HIM ANY TIME SOON!

HE DIDN'T EVEN FIND TIME TO SEND US A CHRISTMAS PRESENT-- EVEN THOUGH WE SENT HIM ONE!

78

IN MY DREAMS, THERE ARE NO UNWANTED BIRTHDAY PARTIES TO PLAN, NO BOY-CRAZY BEST FRIENDS, NO OFF-THE-RAILS OLDER SISTER--

NO BOY-FRIENDS IN LOVE WITH MY TOO-PERFECT TWIN. NO WONDER I'M HOOKED ON BEING THERE. MY DREAM WORLD IS A WHOLE LOT LESS STRESSFUL.

A LITTLE LATER THAT DAY.

SKYE? ARE YOU OK?

I'M SEARCHING FOR CLARA'S LETTERS.

ARE YOU SURE YOU HAVEN'T SEEN THEM?

I DON'T KNOW. COULD MOM HAVE CHUCKED THEM OUT?

I SWEAR, IT'S LIKE YOU'RE OBSESSED! COME DOWNSTAIRS-- WE'RE GOING TO WATCH A MOVIE. MOM'S MADE POPCORN!

DECEMBER 31ST AT MIDNIGHT.

LET'S GO INSIDE. IT'S COLD!

HAPPY NEW YEAR!

I'M GOING TO PLAY THE VIOLIN!

HONEY ISN'T BACK YET?

ARGH!

NO, SHE HAS A ONE O'CLOCK CURFEW!

OK, MY NEW YEAR'S RESOLUTION IS TO TAKE VIOLIN CLASSES WITH PADDY!

YES, AND WE'D BETTER START TOMORROW!

LATER, AFTER MIDNIGHT.

OH, NO! SHE'S PLAYING THAT WRETCHED VIOLIN!

IT'S PAINFUL. MAKE IT GO AWAY!

SUMMER! WHAT'S THAT UNDER YOUR PILLOW?

THE MISSING LETTERS! YOU TOLD ME YOU HADN'T SEEN THEM!

NOT ON PURPOSE! I WAS JUST CURIOUS! YOU'VE BEEN SO OBSESSED WITH STUPID CLARA TRAVERS. IT'S ALL YOU CARE ABOUT!

WHY WOULD YOU LIE?

I WAS WORRIED!

YOU'VE CHANGED, SINCE YOU GOT THOSE STUPID CLOTHES. IT'S SPOOKY, SKYE! I TOOK THEM BECAUSE I WAS WORRIED. YOU SCARE ME WITH YOUR DREAMS!

WE NEVER USED TO HAVE SECRETS!

YOU NEVER USED TO LIE TO ME EITHER!

OK, I SHOULDN'T HAVE TAKEN THE LETTERS, BUT IT'S JUST YOU'RE MORE INTERESTED IN CLARA THAN IN ME LATELY. YOU'RE ALWAYS THINKING ABOUT SOME GIRL WHO'S BEEN DEAD FOR ALMOST A CENTURY. I HATE IT!

YOU USED TO LISTEN TO ME, YOU USED TO NEED ME—

YEAH, THAT'S THE ONLY THING THAT COUNTS, WHATEVER SUMMER WANTS, WHATEVER SUMMER NEEDS.

I HAVE A BAD FEELING. THE SPOOKY STORY, THE LETTERS. AND I HAD A DREAM, TOO!

WHAT KIND OF DREAM?

IT WAS HORRIBLE. I WAS DREAMING ABOUT CLARA TRAVERS, AND SHE WAS WEARING A GREEN DRESS. SHE WAS RUNNING THROUGH THE WOODS, CRYING. I SAW HER FROM BEHIND, LOOKING FOR SOMEONE—AND WHEN SHE TURNED, IT WASN'T CLARA, IT WAS YOU!

AND THEN EVERY-THING CHANGED. YOU WERE UNDERWATER, STRUGGLING, DROWNING. IT WAS HORRIBLE, SKYE!

BUT IT'S NOT REAL, SUMMER. JUST A NIGHTMARE.

IT FELT REAL!

IT FELT LIKE A WARNING! WHAT IF CLARA'S ANGRY AT YOU FOR WEARING HER DRESSES? WHAT IF SHE ACTUALLY DIED IN THAT GREEN DRESS AND IS TRYING TO MAKE YOU DO THE SAME THINGS SHE DID?

WHAT IF SUMMER IS RIGHT? MAYBE I'M IN DANGER?

CLARA DIDN'T DIE IN THE GREEN DRESS, IT WOULDN'T BE HERE IF SHE HAD!

I SUPPOSE. YOU'RE NOT STILL DREAMING ABOUT CLARA?

I CAN'T TELL HER THAT EVERY NIGHT, I AM CLARA TRAVERS.

An odor of marshmallow and of wood floats to me, and the song of a bird pulls me from my slumber

I don't know whether a minute or an hour has passed but when I open my eyes, the trees are green. Even though it's impossible, it doesn't bother me at all. The weather ... pain and ... feel my heart ..., and ... of all but ... are very sweet.

LATE THAT NIGHT.

THESE LETTERS THAT HER FIANCÉ HARRY WROTE. I UNDERSTAND WHY CLARA DIDN'T WANT TO MARRY HIM. HE SOUNDS OVERBEARING AND DEADLY BORING!

I THOUGHT THESE LETTERS WOULD HELP ME UNDERSTAND, BUT THEY'VE DEEPENED THE MYSTERY. POOR CLARA, IF SHE'D MARRIED HARRY, SHE'D HAVE BEEN TRAPPED LIKE A BIRD IN A CAGE!

I NEED TO FIND OUT WH... FINCH IS AND WHY HE'S HAUNTING MY DREAMS.

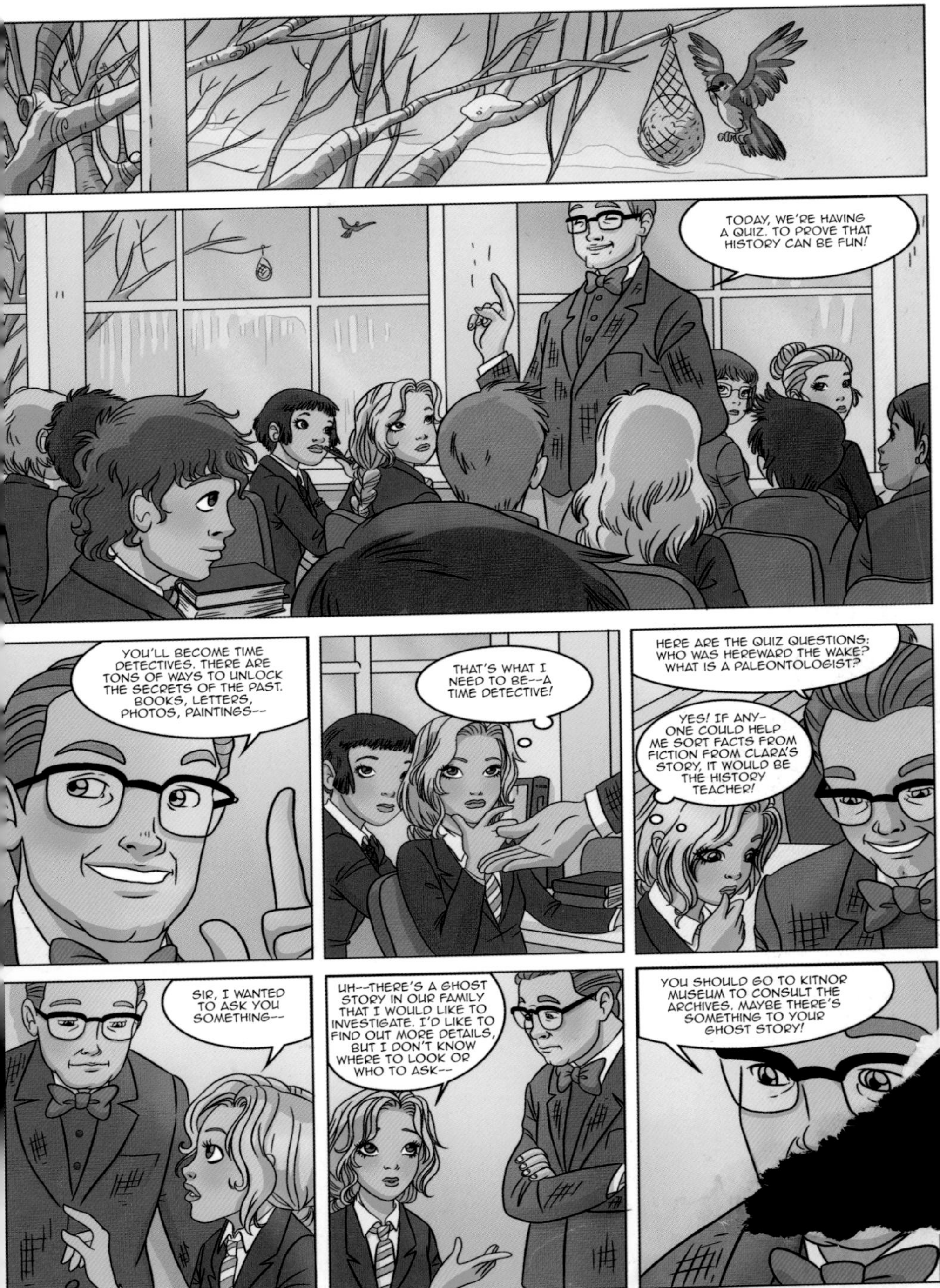
TODAY, WE'RE HAVING A QUIZ. TO PROVE THAT HISTORY CAN BE FUN!
YOU'LL BECOME TIME DETECTIVES. THERE ARE TONS OF WAYS TO UNLOCK THE SECRETS OF THE PAST. BOOKS, LETTERS, PHOTOS, PAINTINGS--
THAT'S WHAT I NEED TO BE--A TIME DETECTIVE!
HERE ARE THE QUIZ QUESTIONS: WHO WAS HEREWARD THE WAKE? WHAT IS A PALEONTOLOGIST?
YES! IF ANY-ONE COULD HELP ME SORT FACTS FROM FICTION FROM CLARA'S STORY, IT WOULD BE THE HISTORY TEACHER!
SIR, I WANTED TO ASK YOU SOMETHING--
UH--THERE'S A GHOST STORY IN OUR FAMILY THAT I WOULD LIKE TO INVESTIGATE. I'D LIKE TO FIND OUT MORE DETAILS, BUT I DON'T KNOW WHERE TO LOOK OR WHO TO ASK--
YOU SHOULD GO TO KITNOR MUSEUM TO CONSULT THE ARCHIVES. MAYBE THERE'S SOMETHING TO YOUR GHOST STORY!

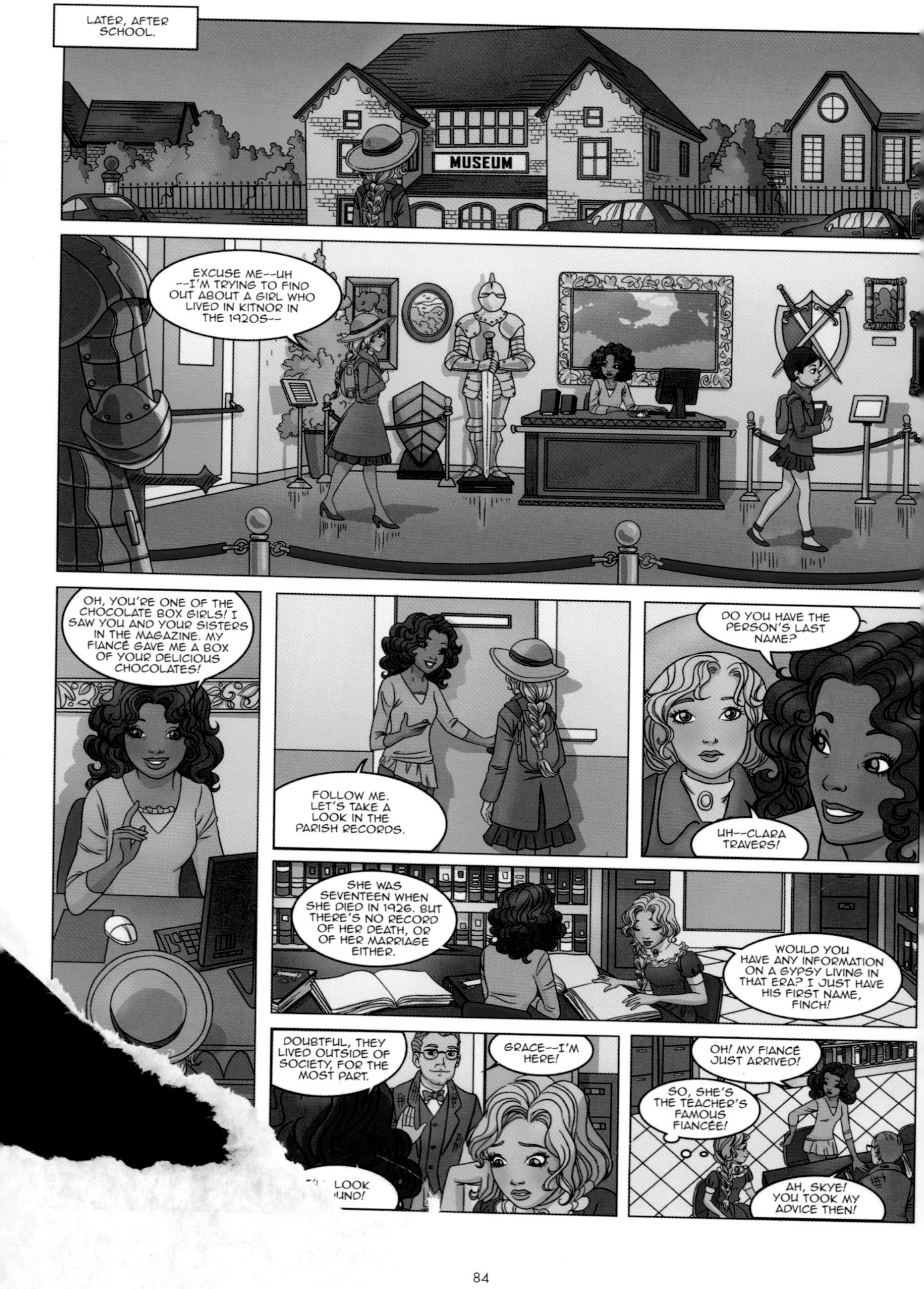

LATER, AFTER SCHOOL.
MUSEUM
EXCUSE ME--UH --I'M TRYING TO FIND OUT ABOUT A GIRL WHO LIVED IN KITNOR IN THE 1920S--
OH, YOU'RE ONE OF THE CHOCOLATE BOX GIRLS! I SAW YOU AND YOUR SISTERS IN THE MAGAZINE. MY FIANCÉ GAVE ME A BOX OF YOUR DELICIOUS CHOCOLATES!
FOLLOW ME. LET'S TAKE A LOOK IN THE PARISH RECORDS.
DO YOU HAVE THE PERSON'S LAST NAME?
UH--CLARA TRAVERS!
SHE WAS SEVENTEEN WHEN SHE DIED IN 1926. BUT THERE'S NO RECORD OF HER DEATH, OR OF HER MARRIAGE EITHER.
WOULD YOU HAVE ANY INFORMATION ON A GYPSY LIVING IN THAT ERA? I JUST HAVE HIS FIRST NAME, FINCH!
DOUBTFUL, THEY LIVED OUTSIDE OF SOCIETY, FOR THE MOST PART.
LOOK
UND!
GRACE--I'M HERE!
OH! MY FIANCÉ JUST ARRIVED!
SO, SHE'S THE TEACHER'S FAMOUS FIANCÉE!
AH, SKYE! YOU TOOK MY ADVICE THEN!

A FEW DAYS LATER.

THURSDAY, THE 14TH OF FEBRUARY. EIGHT TIL LATE-- THE BEST BIRTHDAY PARTY OF THE SEASON!

BRILLIANT!

CAN WE INVITE EVERY-ONE? ALL THE KIDS IN OUR YEAR? AND ALL THE GIRLS FROM THE DANCE SCHOOL?

AND SOME OF THE BOYS FROM THE HIGH SCHOOL?

SKYE? DOES THAT SOUND OK? IT'S YOUR PARTY, TOO!

YEAH--WE COULD DO A VINTAGE THEME!

SKYE! YOU ARE SO HISTORY OBSESSED! HOW ABOUT A VALENTINE THEME?

NOOOO!

I CAN'T WAIT!

COMPROMISE, GIRLS! HOW ABOUT WE MAKE THE THEME "VINTAGE VALENTINE"?

SHAY COULD BE THE DJ!

OKAY, I HAVE TO GO TALK TO HONEY. HER GRADES ARE SLIPPING. IF THIS CONTINUES, I'LL HAVE TO SEND HER TO A BOARDING SCHOOL!

85

I CAN'T WAIT FOR THE PARTY, SUMMER... TO KISS A BOY!

YOU CAN'T GO KISSING BOYS JUST FOR THE SAKE OF IT!

SKYE! WHERE YA GOING?

I HAVE TO GO TO THE MUSEUM. I'M TRYING TO FIND OUT MORE ABOUT CLARA TRAVERS!

COOL, I'LL GO WITH YOU!

SKYE, I FOUND OUT THINGS ABOUT CLARA!

OH! GREAT!

CLARA HAD TWO YOUNGER BROTHERS, CHARLES AND ROBERT, BOTH WERE KILLED IN THE SECOND WORLD WAR. KATE TRAVERS, YOUR GRAN, WAS ROBERT'S ONLY DAUGHTER.

SO CLARA WAS--WHAT, MY GREAT-GREAT-AUNT?

EXACTLY. BUT I FOUND NOTHING ABOUT A PERSON CALLED FINCH!

ON THE OTHER HAND, I FOUND A LETTER SAYING THAT CLARA'S FATHER HAD CHASED THE GYPSIES FROM HIS LANDS!

IT WAS TRUE, THEN, JUST LIKE IN THE STORY.

I'D REALLY LIKE TO KNOW WHO THAT GYPSY FINCH WAS THAT SHE WAS SO IN LOVE WITH!

HOW ABOUT MRS. LEE? SHE'S ALWAYS RATTLING ON ABOUT HOW SHE'S DESCENDED FROM THE ROMANY GYPSIES!

YOU'RE A GENIUS, ALFIE! COME ON! THANKS, GRACE!

SERIOUSLY, HOT CHOCOLATE AND MARSHMALLOWS WOULD BE A MUCH BETTER OPTION.

SKYE! HOW ARE YOU? HOW'S THE ROMANCE GOING?

THERE IS NO ROMANCE. NOT WITH ALFIE. DEFINITELY, ABSOLUTELY NOT!

I'M NOT THAT BAD, AM I? YOU DON'T HAVE TO BE SO QUITE HARSH ABOUT IT.

UH--I WAS ACTUALLY WONDERING--I'M DOING SOME RESEARCH INTO THE GYPSY TRAVELERS. I KNOW YOU'VE GOT TRAVELER BLOOD-- AND I WONDERED--UH--

WELL, MY MOTHER WAS HALF-ROMANY--

SHE WAS BORN IN A VARDO--A BOW-TOP WAGON. SHE DIED TWO OR THREE YEARS BACK NOW. I DO HAVE SOME OLD PHOTOGRAPHS. I'LL TAKE A LOOK FOR YOU.

THANK YOU. I DON'T SUPPOSE--IT'S A MAN NAMED FINCH I AM TRYING TO TRACE. YOU HAVEN'T HEARD OF HIM AT ALL?

I'M SORRY, NO.

LET GO OF IT. LIVE FOR THE MOMENT!

I DO HAVE SOME AUNTS AND UNCLES STILL LIVING, THOUGH. I COULD ASK THEM IF THEY KNOW A CERTAIN FINCH!

THANK YOU. I APPRECIATE THAT. REALLY.

THE FIRST DAY OF WINTER BREAK.

WHAT ARE YOU THINKING ABOUT?

NOTHING!

I CAN'T TELL HER I'M THINKING ABOUT GYPSIES WHO HAD TO LEAVE HURRIEDLY ON A FEBRUARY MORNING BECAUSE OF CLARA'S FATHER!

SNOWBALL FIGHT!

WE'LL WAIT FOR YOU OUTSIDE!

SKYE! PHONE CALL FOR YOU. IT'S ALFIE!

OOO! HER BOYFRIEND!!!

OH! COOL IT, COCO, YOU'RE A PAIN!

DON'T TAKE LONG. A RESEARCHER FOR THE BBC SAW THE MAGAZINE FEATURE ABOUT US. SHE'S RESEARCHING FOR A PERIOD DRAMA ON KITNOR. SHE WANTED TO KNOW ABOUT OUR GYPSY CARAVAN THAT SHE'D NOTICED IN THE MAGAZINE.

SHE'S SUPPOSED TO CALL BACK.

...THE GYPSY CARAVAN?

HI, ALFIE! YEAH. I'D LIKE TO GO SLEDDING THIS AFTERNOON. OK, BYE!

THIS PARTY IS MY BIG CHANCE. IT'S VALENTINE'S DAY. I HAVE TO SHOW SUMMER I'M THE PERFECT BOY FOR HER!

ALFIE, ARE YOU SURE ABOUT THIS?

NEVER SURER!

YOU SHOULD GO OUT WITH MILLIE. SHE'S GETTING QUITE INTERESTED IN BOYS. MORE THAN SUMMER, ANYWAY.

THAT'LL GIVE YOU A CHANCE TO KISS A GIRL. SHE'S TRAINING TO KISS BY SNOGGING THE INSIDE OF HER ELBOW!

NO, THANKS! SUMMER HAS MY HEART!

SUMMER DOESN'T WANT A RELATIONSHIP. SHE'S HUNG UP ON BALLET.

IT'S HER DREAM TO BECOME A PRIMA BALLERINA, AND TRUST ME, IT DOESN'T LEAVE ROOM FOR ROMANCE.

EEEEEEEEEE!

WAHOOOOO!

OWW!

I'M SORRY. ARE YOU OK?

I'D NEVER NOTICED THAT ALFIE ANDERSON HAS THE MOST AMAZING CHOCOLATE-BROWN EYES. ONCE HE STARTED CARESSING MY CHEEK, MY HEART BEAT A LITTLE HARDER. IT FELT VERY STRANGE, BUT NOT ENTIRELY UNPLEASANT. BUT FINCH MAKES MY HEART BEAT FASTER THAN ALFIE EVER COULD.

FEBRUARY 14TH, THE MORNING OF THE BIRTHDAY PARTY.

HAPPY BIRTHDAY, GIRLS!

OH! THANKS, COCO!

I CAME UP WITH A COUPLE OF NEW TRUFFLE IDEAS SPECIALLY FOR YOU TWO-- "MARSHMALLOW SKYE" FOR YOU AND "SUMMER'S DREAM" FOR YOU.

PADDY, THAT'S AMAZING--I LOVE MARSHMALLOW!

I GOT INSPIRED FROM OLD RECIPES BASED ON MARSHMALLOW ROOT AND ROSEWATER!

HAPPY BIRTHDAAAAAY!

WHY ARE YOU WEARING THAT DRESS AND WRAP OF CLARA'S AGAIN?

IT'S MY BIRTHDAY. I CAN WEAR WHAT I LIKE, CAN'T I?

A LITTLE LATER THAT EVENING.

I ASKED SHAY TO PLAY SOME SLOW SONGS! I'M GOING TO ASK SUMMER!

GOOD LUCK!

WANT TO DANCE?

FIFTEEN MINUTES LATER.

I THOUGHT ALFIE WAS IN LOVE WITH YOU?

WHY DO YOU SAY THAT?

THAT'S GROSS!

I FEEL SICK. I SHOULD BE HAPPY FOR ALFIE BUT I JUST FEEL... ALONE.

LOOKS LIKE YOU MISSED YOUR CHANCE THERE! THEY MAKE A GOOD COUPLE, THOUGH. DON'T YOU THINK?

FEEL LIKE VOMITING!

FINCH???

IS HE REAL OR NOT? I DON'T KNOW ANYMORE!

I'M TOTALLY HALLUCINATING.

WHAT'S THIS LETTER?

I'M COLD. I DON'T FEEL WELL.

THE NEXT DAY.

THE SMELL OF THE MARSHMALLOW WOKE ME, SUMMER. I HAD THAT DREAM OF CLARA AGAIN!

YOU REALLY SCARED US YESTERDAY, YOU KNOW!

SKYE, WHEN WE FOUND YOU IN THE SNOW YESTERDAY, YOU WERE HOLDING THIS LETTER IN YOUR HAND! CLARA IS THE ONE WHO WROTE IT!

YES, I FOUND IT IN THE LINING OF THE COAT. THERE WAS A HOLE IN THE POCKET!

ATCHOO! AND I CAUGHT A NICE COLD!

I READ IT. YOU SOLVED THE MYSTERY, YOU KNOW!

I DID?

HARRY, CLARA'S FIANCÉ MUST HAVE NEVER RECEIVED THIS LETTER. SHE EXPLAINS TO HIM SHE DOESN'T LOVE HIM. THAT SHE'S MADLY IN LOVE WITH A GYPSY BOY NAMED SAM—

SAM? BUT IN MY DREAMS, HIS NAME WAS FINCH?

CLARA DIDN'T COMMIT SUICIDE. SHE WRITES THAT SHE'S EXPECTING A CHILD BY SAM. THAT'S SHE'S GOING TO RUN AWAY WITH HIM TO GET MARRIED. SHE'S HAPPY—AND SHE KNOWS SHE'S HURTING HER FAMILY.

I DON'T UNDERSTAND—THE STORIES—WHY?

TO SAVE THE FAMILY NAME? THE SCANDAL OF A RICH MAN'S DAUGHTER WHO GOT PREGNANT OUT OF WEDLOCK AND RAN AWAY WITH THE GYPSIES?

THEY COVERED IT ALL UP, HID AWAY HER THINGS IN A TRUNK!

IT'S LIKE IT WAS ALL MEANT TO HAPPEN, SO YOU'D FIND THE LETTER, SO THE TRUTH WOULD COME OUT!

YOU'VE BEEN MILES AWAY, THESE LAST FEW MONTHS. I'VE BEEN STRESSED OUT AND SELFISH. I REALLY MESSED UP!

YOU DON'T THINK I'M PLAIN AND BORING?

ARE YOU KIDDING ME, SKYE? TRUST ME, YOU'RE THE MOST INTERESTING PERSON I KNOW. YOU'RE COOL AND CREATIVE.

I LOVE YOU!

I LOVE YOU, TOO, LITTLE SISTER!

A FEW DAYS LATER.

I PROMISED I'D TAKE OUT MOM'S PICTURES OF THE OLD DAYS. LOOK WHAT I FOUND!

THE BABY-- THAT'S MY MOTHER!

HER NAME WAS LIN, FOR LINNET. THOSE ARE MY GRANDPARENTS.

A LINNET IS A FINCH. THAT'S IT! AND WHAT WERE YOUR GRANDPARENTS' NAMES?

SAM COOPER, MY GRANDAD WAS CALLED. AND JANE.

JANE!!! JUST LIKE CLARA TRAVERS' MIDDLE NAME. CLARA JANE TRAVERS. AND SAM--LIKE HER LOVER!

SO YOUR GRAND-MOTHER IS MY GREAT-GREAT-AUNT CLARA TRAVERS. IT'S CRAZY! UNBELIEVABLE!

I CANNOT QUITE WORK OUT WHERE FINCH FIT IN. THE BOY IN MY DREAMS LOOKED NOTHING LIKE CLARA'S LOVE. MAYBE HE WAS JUST MY IMAGINATION'S VERSION OF A COOL GYPSY BOY? IT WAS A FANTASY, A PERFECT ROMANCE CONJURED UP BY A GIRL WHO WASN'T QUITE READY FOR A REAL-LIFE BOYFRIEND. WHO KNOWS?

TWO WEEKS LATER.

I'M GETTING USED TO THE FACT THAT SUMMER IS GOING OUT WITH AARON JONES, AND MILLIE IS NO LONGER INTERESTED IN ALFIE. SHE GOT HER FIRST KISS. POOR ALFIE IS STILL PINING FOR SUMMER.

HELLO, I'M NIKKI, THE RESEARCHER. I HAVE AN APPOINTMENT WITH YOUR MOTHER!

OH! YOU'RE HERE ABOUT LOCATION SCOUTING, RIGHT?

YES. WE'RE GOING TO SHOOT A PERIOD DRAMA BASED ON THE LIFE OF GYPSIES WHO LIVED HERE SOME YEARS AGO. AND WE'RE INTERESTED IN YOUR CARAVAN!

YOUR MOTHER TOLD ME THE STORY ON THE PHONE OF YOUR ANCESTOR CLARA TRAVERS. GREAT STUFF!

OH! YES!

SEE YOU SOON!

A HALF-HOUR LATER.

FRED, COME ON. LET'S GO HOME!

UH--HEY!

I THINK NIKKI IS AT YOUR HOUSE. I HAVE TO JOIN HER. SHE'S MY MOM.

OH--YES. SHE'S IN THE HOUSE.

MY NAME'S JAMIE--JAMIE FINCH.

FINCH! SO-- HE'S THE BOY OF MY DREAMS!

THE END OF PART 2 "THE GYPSY GHOST"

Welcome to

I am definitely obsessed with all things romance. It's fun, it's dramatic, and it's all about love. I think love is pretty amazing, don't you? When your heart beats faster at the sound of someone else's voice or the way they smile, you just feel more alive. And terrified! Or how about when just being around that special someone makes you feel like you're flying? Like you could do anything? Falling in love is one of the most incredible feelings, ever.

Of course, love is also complicated and painful sometimes. They don't call them "crushes" for nothing!

Yet, when I'm feeling kind of meh or sad, the first thing I want to do is read a romance. Maybe it's because everyone falls in love, has heartbreak and heartache. Maybe it's because there's really nothing like your first kiss. Whatever the reason, when I want to feel better, I pick up a romance and settle in. Usually with tea and chocolate, if I'm being totally honest.

Which brings us to Charmz, a new line of graphic novels just for you! With stories from all over the world, Charmz wants to celebrate love. Whether we're hanging out in Somerset, UK, the wilds of France, speeding through space, or waking up in a cemetery, love finds our characters and digs right in.

Whether you're in the mood for a (literally!) sweet tale about sisters, chocolate, and forbidden love, or exploring the mysterious darkness of Assumption Cemetery where vampires and swamp boys romance stitched girls, you'll find a lot to relate to.

My favorite kinds of romance are epic, sweeping, and probably just a little bit hilarious. As seriously as I take love, if you don't laugh a little at the things we'll do for it, well, you'll end up actually lovesick. Which is definitely something the girls in our books have to deal with from time to time. Not to mention fashion faux pas, weird chocolate recipes, ghosts, zombie sheep, and puzzles through time and space!

I've read a lot of romances and I definitely have my favorites. I think the one I would take on a desert island would have to be *Pride and Prejudice* by Jane Austen. I know, it's old, but it's so witty, and funny, and real. It's been adapted so many times but it always feels fresh and relevant. Anyone could be those characters. Me. You.

Aside from editing this line of graphic novels, I'm also writing one: STITCHED. This spooky little cemetery book with vampires, werewolves, swamp boys and stitched girls is very dear to me. It's the book I've always wanted to write, with spectacularly weird creatures, spooky adventures, and lots and lots of awkward, splendid, romance. Crimson Volania Mulch is my favorite kind of girl; complicated, smart, curious, kind...but a little bit preoccupied with her own problems. And way too judgmental. No one is perfect! And if I woke up only knowing my name in a strange place, I might be a little self-involved, too. I mean, just who is that pretty boy she meets on her first night "alive," and where is her mother? What does a badger/hedgehog actually eat? Do werewolves like cupcakes?

What I want Charmz to be for you is like the book equivalent of a hot chocolate; sweet, maybe a little dark sometimes, comforting, and made just for you. You can curl up with our tales, settle in, and enjoy falling in love with our characters just like they fall in love with each other.

Remember: stories matter, love is powerful, and there's nothing like a love story to make you feel alive.

–Mariah McCourt

Please write to me any time about Charmz! mariah@papercutz.com

I would love hear from you.

STAY IN TOUCH!

EMAIL: charmz@papercutz
WEB: www.papercutz.com
TWITTER: @papercutzgn
FACEBOOK: PAPERCUTZGRAPHICNOVELS
REGULAR MAIL: Charmz, 160 Broadway, Suite 700, East Wing, New York, NY 10038